KATE PROCTOR

The Price of Desire

Harlequin Books

TORONTO • NEW YORK • LONDON
AMSTERDAM • PARIS • SYDNEY • HAMBURG
STOCKHOLM • ATHENS • TOKYO • MILAN
MADRID • WARSAW • BUDAPEST • AUCKLAND

Harlequin Presents first edition January 1993
ISBN 0-373-11526-1

Original hardcover edition published in 1991
by Mills & Boon Limited

THE PRICE OF DESIRE

CHAPTER ONE

THE disadvantage in arriving so early for her appointment with Alexander Carmichael's son, mused Cassandra Lestor with a sinking feeling, was the amount of time it left for thought. And the trouble with thinking was the inevitable drift of her thoughts, no matter how she tried to side-track them; a drift that would soon have her a nervous wreck with its reflections on the futility of her original optimism.

She took a deep breath, pursing lips that were full and strikingly sensuous in contrast to the rest of her classically proportioned features. Fatalistically accepting that there wasn't the remotest chance that any amount of deep breathing would calm her, she began smoothing her hands nervously against the faded denim of her skirt—an action that unfortunately reminded her just how inappropriately dressed she must seem for what she desperately hoped would turn out to be a job interview with a man she now knew to be considered one of the most influential and ruthless in the entire business arena of Europe.

She gave a small grimace of despair, her hands reaching up in a gesture of nervous reflex to smooth back the dark blonde hair hanging heavily against her shoulders, while her thoughts gloomily informed her that at least now she was seeing things realistically... by all the laws of recent experience, the odds were on things getting worse rather than better.

Then her hands returned to clasp her smoothly tanned knees as she remonstrated with herself for wallowing in self-pity. The man she was getting herself so tied up in knots at the thought of meeting had also recently lost his father—and had doubtless loved him every bit as much as she had hers. And it had to be the ghastly turmoil into which her own father's death three months previously had thrown both her life and that of her sister that had rendered her incapable of reacting in anything but purely selfish terms to hearing of Alexander Carmichael's death. Not that she had known him particularly well, she reminded herself defensively. But she had felt completely at ease with him—which was more than could be said for her feelings towards his son, also Alexander, whom she had once fleetingly met over a year ago.

'Cassandra, this is my elder son, Sacha.' Alexander Carmichael's words leapt from the recesses of her memory. 'My late wife decided on the diminutive Sacha when she realised two Alexanders in the same household might present a few communication problems.'

Cassandra gave an involuntary shiver, experiencing yet again that irrational stab of premonitory fear she had felt as she had then returned Sacha Carmichael's perfunctory handshake. She had few doubts that those cold grey-blue eyes had taken in little or nothing of the gauche student over whom they had so cursorily swept.

He had been in a hurry, she remembered—citing a business appointment as his excuse. But Cassandra had gained the impression that his rush had more to do with escaping the company of the woman who had waylaid him only a few seconds before his father had spotted him.

It was strange how certain impressions could be formed on so little, she thought with a frown, and yet remain fixed so solidly in the mind...as in the case of her fleeting encounter with Sacha Carmichael. The sensation of the power exuding from him had struck her with an extraordinary force, as though power were a commodity over which he held exclusive franchise. It had been there in the tall, broad-shouldered leanness of his magnificently proportioned body; and there also in the striking, harshly masculine beauty of looks that would inevitably draw the lingering attention of the majority of women. And the attention of the outstandingly lovely woman by his side had been exclusively on him, she remembered. Though completely ignorant of such matters, she had had the peculiar sensation of her mind tuning in to the rejection felt by that woman as Sacha Carmichael had removed her hand from his arm in a gesture of cold rebuff.

As she remembered she realised how completely illogical it was for her to harbour such feelings of antagonism towards the man she was about to meet—for antagonism it undoubtedly was, she admitted uncomfortably—on the strength of those groundless impressions gained in the space of mere seconds.

'Mr Carmichael will see you now,' the immaculately groomed receptionist lifted her head to inform her.

Cassandra rose to her feet, feeling gauche and scruffy and, for the first time in her life, completely bereft of anything even approaching self-confidence as it came to her with a frightening finality that, though her mind might have been developed to its highest capacity, in terms of the normal requirements of society she was pitiably ignorant.

Yet there was a strength in her, as she closed the door behind her, that suppressed her inner turmoil to no more than a hint of wariness in the wide-spaced blue eyes that met those of the man rising from a huge carved desk.

He was in shirt-sleeves, his undone tie hanging dark and untidy against the sharp whiteness of his shirt. And to that same aura of power she had so accurately recalled there was now added an almost animal vitality exuding from him; a vitality curiously at variance with the unexpectedly graceful indolence of his movements as he approached and stretched out a hand to her.

'You must be Cassandra,' he stated in minimal greeting.

'And you must be Sacha,' she replied, catching the momentary disapproval in the reflex widening of his shrewd grey-blue eyes as she returned his brief, firm handshake. 'We met once before,' she added, and was instantly irritated with herself. Why should she have felt the need to offer an explanation for what he so clearly considered a liberty on her part—he had used her Christian name, so where was the wrong in her using his?

Without making any false claims to recalling having met her—a point she would have found admirable in others but could only see as arrogance in this man she decidedly disliked, no matter how illogical—he returned to his desk and motioned her to be seated.

Dislike him or not, there were certain courtesies to be observed, which she did as she sat down. 'I was very sorry to hear about your father.'

'So you mentioned in your letter,' he stated with a brusqueness she felt it only fair to put down to the pain of loss as he referred to the letter she had sent him in reply to his tersely informative response to her original letter to his father. 'What exactly was it you wished to see my father about?' he continued, rattling her with a glance he gave to the wafer-thin gold watch nestling against the dark hairs of his wrist.

'I was going to ask him to give me a job,' she replied, her tone succinctly reflecting her displeasure at his display of what she considered to be a lack of manners.

The dark, elegant curve of his brows rose a censuring fraction.

The look in Cassandra's eyes, as they met his, was now candidly challenging. He had asked the question and she had done no more than answer it, she told herself, while at the same time mentally writing off any chance of employment in any part of the vast Carmichael empire—least of all in that tiny part of it in which she had once felt so at home.

'Really? I was under the impression your employment here had already been arranged,' he muttered, reaching for a file on the desk-top. He opened the file, which she realised must be hers, his eyes skimming rapidly over its introductory page.

'Yes, it has. But...' She fell silent as he held up a peremptory hand and continued to read.

It was all probably double Dutch to him, she thought resignedly. While his was undoubtedly the brain behind the rest of the huge family business, the esoteric section of the Carmichael empire, specialising in the translation of academic tracts and with which she had become involved, had been his father's exclusive concern. And, to her, the rarefied atmosphere of that section had seemed like home from home. Only the hope of working there had rendered more tolerable the daunting years that lay ahead of her, when her role was to be little more than slave to the crippling burden of debt now overshadowing both her life and that of her sister Helen.

He snapped shut the file, a faint gleam of derision in his eyes as he recited some of her academic achievements—considerable ones, given her youth.

'And at the moment you're in the throes of a PhD in Classical Greek at Athens——'

'Exactly what do you mean, "in the throes"?' she burst out, stung to recklessness by the open mockery in his tone.

'It just strikes me that you appear to be something of a compulsive student,' he retorted. 'In fact, I'm surprised you managed to squeeze in working here at all— I'd have thought you'd be busy cramming in your holidays.'

Cassandra leapt to her feet, rage and hopelessness draining the colour from her face. 'It's best if I waste no more of your obviously precious time, Mr Carmichael, nor mine either——'

'Rest assured, Miss Lestor, you'd have been shown the door instantly had there been any danger of my time being wasted,' he interrupted silkily. 'But as for yours— it was you who wished to see me, not I you.' His eyes caught and held hers in mocking challenge. 'And now I suggest you count to ten, or whatever it is you do to get to grips with that rather short temper of yours.'

He leaned back in his chair, waiting, his entire demeanour a parody of good-natured patience as pride and common sense waged savage battle within Cassandra.

At last she returned to her seat, common sense winning as it had to. As he had been so quick to point out, Sacha Carmichael was not a man given to time-wasting, and the mere fact that she was still in his office had to be a cause for some measure of hope. And as for pride, it was a luxury she had to forgo in her single-minded pursuit of the money she and Helen so desperately needed.

'Now where was I?' he murmured, as though her capitulation had always been a foregone conclusion. 'You're to join the company permanently when the Alcaeus manuscripts are released for translation . . . which appears to coincide neatly with the completion of your PhD.'

'That's the point I'm trying to make—I shan't be completing it,' she exclaimed. 'Mr Carmichael——'

'You started off with Sacha, so why not continue?' he cut in abruptly, opening up the file and perusing it once more. 'Carmichael's will have a team working exclusively on the Alcaeus project,' he recited as he found what he was looking for, 'liaising with Cambridge under the direction of their Professor William Lestor. Any relation?'

'My father,' replied Cassandra tonelessly. 'But he died recently.'

For an instant the cold guardedness on his handsome features was transformed by the naked honesty of compassion. 'I'm sorry to hear that, Cassandra, I truly am,' he murmured, his tone betraying just how deeply the death of his own father must have affected him. 'But I'm sure the last thing he'd have wanted was for you to give up your studies.'

Cassandra glanced down at her hands, now clenched tightly in her lap. Until she had mentioned her father's death his attitude to her studies had been openly derisive.

'I'm giving up for other reasons,' she stated evasively, refusing to play on what she suspected might be the one chink in his abrasive armour. Intuition told her there was something she had that Sacha Carmichael needed, though what it could possibly be she had no idea. And another thing that intuition was strongly telling her was that genuine though his feelings of sympathy towards her might be, they would never in a month of Sundays lead to his offering her a job on the strength of them. She took a deep breath as yet another thought occurred to her. 'I think I should point out that I was to join the Carmichael Alcaeus team on my merits alone—not because of any involvement of my father's.'

'It hadn't occurred to me to think otherwise,' he drawled, snapping shut the file as all trace of compassion deserted his features. 'Are you always this damned sensitive?'

Once again she leapt to her feet—a purely reflex action. She had had more than enough of this obnoxious man's sneering arrogance!

'Look, if you intend bobbing up and down like a Yo-Yo, would you mind doing it in someone else's time? If not, sit down and stay there until we've finished.'

Knowing she had no choice, but not trusting herself to speak for fear of what came out, Cassandra resumed her seat.

'So—tell me something about this Alcaeus business. Other than its having sent Greek scholars into a spin, I know next to nothing about it.'

Having managed to blank her mind in order to cope with an ordeal that was becoming more nightmarish with every passing second, Cassandra now found herself battling against reaction to what she could only regard as a blatant lie. She knew how delighted Alexander Carmichael had been about the manuscripts, and of one thing she was completely sure: no son of his, especially not one who had loved him as this man undoubtedly had, could have remained in ignorance of even the slightest detail pertaining to that subject which so thrilled him.

'Surely you know something about them,' he probed in silky tones that reflected nothing of the impatience now gleaming openly in his eyes.

Cassandra mentally kicked herself for her own stupidity—he was obviously testing her knowledge, though to what end she couldn't begin to imagine. Her anger and frustration augmented by the insulting blatancy of his ploy, she found herself adopting a vocabulary geared towards a not too bright ten-year-old as she proceeded to tell him all she knew.

'Before you continue,' he interrupted, soon after she had begun, 'I should explain that words of more than one syllable won't leave me floundering.' The tone was mild, but again it was the eyes that spelled out the warning.

And this time she heeded the warning with alacrity. It was intuition and precious little else that told her he might have some use in mind for her. But the unpleasant fact to be faced was that if it came down to grovelling to get herself a job in the only workplace into which she knew with certainty she could fit, then grovelling would be her sole option.

With these unpalatable facts starkly in mind, she began speaking again. And after a while there came a change in her, gradual yet dramatic, as she became immersed in a subject that transported her back to the life that had so recently been hers. A life idyllic and uncomplicated, where the material world had never encroached, where she had been free to be herself and where, too, caution and uncertainty, now her constant companions, had been virtual strangers.

Sacha Carmichael listened in silence. He watched as the mask slipped gradually from her face and saw that face transformed by spontaneous vivacity to a remarkable and strangely moving beauty.

'There's so much to be excited about,' she exclaimed, unwittingly smiling as she ran slim fingers through the tawny mass of her hair in an unconscious gesture of freedom, completely lost in her subject. 'Of course, whether or not this turns out to be the work of the same Alcaeus Homer so admired remains to be discovered—though computer analysis will make the assessment much simpler.' She broke off, suddenly inordinately aware of his silent scrutiny. 'I'm sorry,' she muttered stiltedly, mortified by the extent to which she had allowed herself to become carried away.

'Why apologise?' he asked. 'You've made it all sound most interesting.'

Those words wiped away the last traces of enthusiasm from her face. His continued pretence of ignorance left her feeling dejected and deflated, and she watched in wary silence as he rose suddenly and stretched with the lazy abandon of a huge cat. He then raked absent-minded fingers through the unruly mahogany darkness of his hair before placing his hands on the desktop, his broad shoulders tensing slightly as he gazed down at the blotter before him with a look of total concentration.

'You're—what—twenty-three?' he eventually demanded from the blue.

'Twenty-four at the beginning of December,' she replied, a faint hope she was loath to trust taking root in her.

He flung his large frame back on to the chair, his expression still one of total concentration as his body lazily swung the chair from side to side.

'Carmichael's is one of the largest and also one of the most diversified organisations in Europe,' he stated in a curiously expressionless voice. 'We have strongholds in fields as diverse as pharmaceuticals and precision engineering.' He broke off, his glance impaling hers. 'Not that such information would be of the slightest interest to you.' He gave the ghost of a smile as Cassandra made a hasty attempt to adopt a look of avid interest and failed. 'I thought not,' he murmured, his tone, to her increasing bemusement, sounding almost satisfied. 'It was only six years ago that my father decided to turn the company over to my control—bar, of course, that one section that had always held such a unique place in his affections.'

Cassandra was unable to mask her astonishment. While she could see the man before her in no role other than that of high-powered and ruthless tycoon, it was one she could never for the life of her envisage his father in, despite the vague realisation, somewhere at the back of her mind, that Alexander Carmichael was probably the sole proprietor of the vast organisation bearing his name.

'But he was a typical classics scholar,' she blurted out.

'Typical to whom?' he drawled chillingly. 'I take it your vision of a classics scholar is of one above dirtying his hands in the business arena.'

'That isn't what I meant at all,' she protested, though uncertain in her own mind as to what she had meant.

He gave an abruptly dismissive shrug before continuing. 'My mother's death shortly before had a lot to do with his decision.' He hesitated, as though searching for words, the accompanying look of irritation on his face exhibiting just how unused he was to having to choose his words with such care. 'That work became his whole life...but recent ill health had forced him into looking around for someone he could eventually hand over to. As luck would have it, he found the ideal person.' This time, when he broke off, Cassandra swiftly lowered her eyes as she glimpsed the naked grief in his. Sacha Carmichael, she realised intuitively, was not a man who went in for baring his emotions. 'As was to be expected of someone of the calibre my father was seeking, this man had commitments, and it will be some time before he's free to...to assume my father's role.'

Cassandra's eyes had risen once again at the sound of that uncharacteristic hesitation. The heavy scowl now darkening those extraordinarily handsome features only served to underline her conviction that she was witnessing a man caught in a dilemma, the results of which were causing him to behave in a way completely alien to a nature that was forceful and uncompromising.

'I take it that you're aware that, though the section is commonly referred to as "the Tower", its correct name is Carmichael Bower?' he demanded suddenly. 'Professor Eric Bower being the man who introduced the original concept to my grandfather.'

'The Tower of Babel,' murmured Cassandra incautiously, remembering the twinkle in Alexander Carmichael's eyes when telling her of the name the rest of the company had dubbed it almost from the start, before time had eventually shortened it simply to the Tower.

'Well, Tower of Babel is what it's in danger of deteriorating into, unless I can get things straightened out pretty damned quick.'

Cassandra regarded him with appalled disbelief.

'Though the rest of the company finances the Tower, I had nothing whatsoever to do with any part of it, and now, even though I've had a team of company accountants go over the records, the amount of light we've been able to shed is minimal.'

'The amount of light shed on what?' asked Cassandra, totally out of her depth. She had absolutely no idea what any of this confusing jumble could possibly have to do with her.

'On the way the section operates,' he exclaimed impatiently. 'Apart from a handful of permanent staff, it all seems to revolve round a hotchpotch of eggheads. Some appear to be called in on a periodic consultancy basis, others are paid retainers and others...' He broke off with an exclamation of frustration, slamming his hand down on her file. 'For example, the files are impeccably kept as far as qualifications and work done for the Tower go—hence yours. But contracts, rates of pay— in fact all the information needed to keep the department running at its most basic level, aren't duplicated from the computer files on to any of them.'

Cassandra gave him a wary look, her complete ignorance of such procedures precluding her from even detecting the problem he obviously saw as glaring. 'What about Mrs Jessel, your father's assistant?' she offered diffidently.

'Mrs Jessel is part of the problem,' he exclaimed, dragging impatient fingers through his hair. 'She soldiered on for a few months after my father died...as far as we all were concerned, Mrs Jessel would be there to show the new man the ropes when he arrived, pretty much as my father would have. Unfortunately, and, in retrospect, most thoughtlessly, none of us realised the effect his death had had on her.' He paused to pick up a lacquered pen and began passing it back and forth between his hands. Cassandra found herself watching, completely mesmerised by the movements of those strong, darkly tanned hands, their long, tapering fingers flexing with delicate sureness as they handled the pen. 'She walked into my office late one Friday afternoon and announced that she was retiring—with immediate effect.'

Cassandra was startled, finding it impossible to equate so seemingly irresponsible an action with the calm, efficient woman she remembered.

'I was as surprised then as you obviously are now,' he remarked quietly, returning the pen to the blotter. 'But, in a very short space of time, I realised I wasn't talking to the Mildred Jessel who had been like an extension of my father's right hand...I was talking to a slightly dotty old lady.' He glanced up at Cassandra's sharp intake of breath. 'Did you realise she was almost seventy?'

Cassandra shook her head, unable to speak. Though she didn't claim to be a particularly good judge, she would probably have placed Mildred Jessel at no more than in her late fifties.

'None of us did...but she looked every year of it that day. Perhaps, had she been younger, Dad's death wouldn't have knocked the stuffing out of her quite as it ultimately did. Fortunately, her health's good, and he left her a considerable amount of money.'

'But the running of the Tower—she would have had all that at her fingertips,' said Cassandra.

'Yes—except that by the time that fact had been brought to my attention and I got around to asking for her assistance, I realised that her business mind had retired along with her body...I'm afraid I drew a blank with her.'

'Maybe someone she knew better...' began Cassandra, her words petering away as she realised they could be interpreted as implying criticism—which of course they were; there was little of Alexander Carmichael's gentle charm evident in his son.

'Believe it or not, I don't go in for browbeating defenceless old ladies,' Sacha remarked with a faint glimmer of amusement. 'Just accept the fact that, for one reason or another, I've been left in a position I find invidious. And another fact to be accepted is that my father had one of the sharpest business brains there is, and no matter what it was he was running it would have been administered with the same meticulous detail as he once applied to this entire organisation.'

'I'm sure you're right,' said Cassandra, then took a deep breath as she decided to take the bull by the horns. 'You obviously have your reasons for asking me here and telling me all this—but I can't even begin to guess what they are.'

'I had very definite reasons, but meeting you has led me to re-evaluate them considerably.'

It had only been a small chance to start with, thought Cassandra dejectedly, but what little there had been she had blown by antagonising him. Perhaps, had she had any idea how to handle people... but now she would never know. And now, worst of all, she would have to ring Helen with nothing but more bad news.

'What about the Alcaeus project?' she asked tonelessly. She would be prepared to earn money digging roads for the next eighteen months, if only she had the Alcaeus project to look forward to.

'That's one thing that worries me,' he stated, his words sending her heart plummeting to the depths. 'Forgive me for my bluntness, but won't your father's death have repercussions on the project?'

'None,' intoned Cassandra. 'He considered being offered it the supreme accolade, as will anyone else in his field who is now approached. And as for speaking bluntly,' she added, 'it's the only method of communication I'm entirely at home with.'

'Something I shall bear in mind in my future dealings with you,' he informed her, a cold edge to the softness of his words.

Cassandra flashed him a look that was both questioning and hostile.

'I was clutching at straws when I asked you here—is that blunt enough for you?'

'Yes,' she said.

'In my original optimism I put feelers out to some of those I knew had had connections with the Tower and discovered that, on a business level, I might just as well have been consulting people from another planet. Then I skimmed through your file and found someone who had worked there and had the necessary academic background, yet someone young enough to have at least one foot still on this planet...someone who, in my desperation, I hoped might have a few suggestions as to the type of person necessary to keep the Tower ticking over on an interim basis.'

'Why on earth didn't you simply explain all that when I first walked in?' exclaimed Cassandra, her irritation evident. She had been invited here merely to help someone else get a job!

'Perhaps it's just as well I didn't, as I've now decided to offer you the position.'

'Me?' Cassandra almost shrieked.

'As a last resort I could have called in several teams of experts, but that delicate network of brain-power that constitutes the essence of the Tower and which my father understood so well . . . how could I guarantee it wouldn't be irrevocably damaged?'

'So how could you possibly contemplate entrusting it to me?' gasped Cassandra, the fact that she was talking herself out of a job no longer even a consideration.

'Because you know the type of people you would have to deal with as few others of your age would. And because you have a vested interest in the Alcaeus project, which would have to be undertaken elsewhere if the Tower was to collapse.'

'If I were capable of doing what you ask—which I don't for one moment think I am—I'd not require a vested interest,' she retorted hotly, shocked by what she saw as his total lack of values. 'But the point is, I've absolutely no idea how any business, let alone that of the Tower, operates!'

'You know what tipped me over into offering you the job?' he asked blandly, totally disregarding her outburst. 'It was something I'd overlooked earlier on your file—your computer experience.' He paused then, for the first time since she had entered the room, he actually smiled.

It was a smile that for one instant left her bemused and thoroughly disarmed, and which, in the next, brought the ludicrous thought to her head that he was well advised to ration such a smile as strictly as he did because, given the right time and the right place, its consequences could probably be quite devastating. And it was in the third instant after he had unleashed the power of that smile that she realised he had paused merely to continue, and she had missed every subsequent word he had uttered.

'I'm sorry...I didn't catch what you said,' she stammered, horrified to feel the hot colour racing to her cheeks.

'I asked why you'd undergone such an intensive computer course when your field is obviously languages.'

Acutely conscious of her heightened colour and the gaze of those shrewd eyes that missed nothing, she told him of how she had once helped her father in establishing the authenticity of a work attributed to Homer.

'I had first-hand experience of the vital role played by computer technology in such an area and decided a working knowledge might be useful,' she explained. 'As my father held the chair in classics at Harvard at the time, it was only natural that I should take a course there.'

'Only natural,' he echoed, his words tinged with amusement. 'But to get back to the point,' he continued briskly. 'I own this company for no other reason than that I'm my father's son. But its continued, not to mention increasing, power and success is down to my business acumen. When I admit to being pushed into clutching at straws regarding the Tower I should, nevertheless, point out that my business instincts tell me that together we stand a far better than average chance of coming up trumps.'

'Together?' Cassandra croaked, her thought processes barely functioning.

'Most definitely together,' he declared decisively. 'For one thing, finding myself in a state of ignorance regarding a section of my own company, as I have in recent months, is something I have no intention of letting occur a second time; and, for another, although I intend giving you what many would regard as a uniquely free hand, it will be a hand guided solely by my understanding and acceptance of your goals; and, lastly, the irritating cause of the most immediate of our problems, namely lack of access to the computer files, is something I've a feeling you're more likely to stand a chance of solving than most.'

She continued to look at him with blank incomprehension.

'My father had a penchant for playing intellectual games when assigning code names to documents, which makes life somewhat impossible for the average computer clerk who hasn't a list of those codes, wouldn't you say?'

The ghost of an impish smile flitted across Cassandra's face.

'So...do we now start thrashing out a contract of employment, or what?'

CHAPTER TWO

CASSANDRA awoke early and troubled the morning she was to start work at Carmichael's. But her leaden limbs and the stomach-churning sensation of gloom assailing her had more to do with her telephone conversation with Helen the previous Friday than the daunting prospect of the day before her.

The fact that the thousands of miles separating them would inevitably remain there between them for the next several years was something that lay heavy and unacknowledged in their infrequent conversations. Yet there had been pleasure and relief in Helen's voice when she had learned of the job, and comfort in her gentle words of wisdom as she had stemmed her younger sister's unintended outpouring of doubt and anxiety.

Cassandra sat down on the edge of the bed, her mind filled with the gentle presence of her sister. She had been barely three when their mother had died of a rare and virulent viral infection, but she had never been conscious of being overwhelmed by the gap created by that tragic happening. William Lestor had always been the most attentive of fathers, but most of all there had been Helen—four years her senior and blessed, even in early childhood, with a sweetness and maturity beyond her years.

But on Friday she had detected something unfamiliar behind Helen's words of congratulations and encouragement—something that had disturbed her deeply despite her inability to define it any concrete way.

Her mind still preoccupied, she cast a dubious eye over her meagre wardrobe, then selected a straight, pale khaki skirt and black T-shirt and dressed.

She was brushing her hair, muttering impatiently to herself when its blonde thickness refused to be tamed, when it came to her what it was she had heard in her sister's voice—an underlying note she now recognised as despair.

Scarcely bothering to check her appearance, she slipped on a pair of black leather pumps and left the house—it was a fair walk to Carmichael's, but she had no intention of squandering money on public transport.

As she walked along in the fresh morning air she remembered the lie she had told Helen—the first she could ever recall telling her—and felt no shame for her deceit. Because of the enormity of the amount they owed and the consequently horrifying amount of interest accumulating with each year it remained outstanding, she had considerably inflated the sum of the already generous salary Sacha Carmichael had offered her, knowing Helen would let their debt drag on rather than subject her younger sister to the same financial hardships she had imposed on herself. But the true irony was in her knowing precisely what her sister earned, and therefore the full extent of that hardship, because her own first lie to Helen had been no more than a repetition of Helen's to her.

Bracing her slim shoulders, she swung open one of the heavy plate glass doors and entered the building. It surprised her to find that her name was familiar to the security guard who approached her and asked for it. But she was reproaching herself for the naïveté of her surprise as she entered the lift; such attention to detail was no more than to be expected in a business controlled by a man such as Sacha Carmichael.

And it was with feelings more in line with those of an early Christian martyr than a confident new employee that she entered the suite of offices from which Sacha Carmichael wielded his awesome power.

'Hello—I'm Cassandra Lestor.' With a diffident smile she addressed the receptionist she recognised from Friday. 'I'm a bit early—is Sacha Carmichael here yet?'

Cool eyes in a flawlessly made up face took in Cassandra's casual attire.

'I'll have a word with Mr Carmichael's secretary,' murmured the girl, picking up a receiver and tapping numbers on to the complicated-looking keyboard before her. 'Lisa, there's a Miss Lestor here to see Mr Carmichael.' She listened for several seconds, her face a remote mask, then replaced the receiver. 'Mr Carmichael's secretary will see you shortly.'

Cassandra considered for a moment pointing out that his secretary was not the person she had asked to see, before deciding that such a statement of fact might be misinterpreted. Then she found herself wondering if perfect looks and grooming, together with an air of cool detachment, were mandatory for the company's female staff as a tall brunette glided into sight, the same faintly judgemental expression in the eyes flickering over the visitor as had been in those of the receptionist.

'I'm Lisa Hampton, can I help you?' asked the girl as she reached the reception desk.

'I'd like to see Sacha Carmichael,' replied Cassandra.

'Mr Carmichael is having a business breakfast,' stated Lisa Hampton, her eyes flickering towards those of the receptionist, then quickly away as she gave barely perceptible emphasis to her employer's courtesy title.

The almost ritualistic formality of the exchange, together with its subtle nuances of censure, filled

Cassandra with foreboding. There was no hope of her ever fitting in with people like this, she thought despondently, remembering her father's scathing observations on the superficiality and dishonesty of a world of which he wanted no part. But she was to be well and truly part of it now—a world that would no doubt regard her as a complete misfit and one which she still found herself observing with the nervous fascination of a visiting alien. Then, with a sudden flash of impatience with herself for being so uncharacteristically negative, she cast her despondency aside and took a deep breath.

'He asked me to——'

'Good morning, ladies.' Sacha Carmichael's words brought immediate life to his two languid employees.

The receptionist beamed him a smile of which Cassandra would have suspected those frozen facial muscles incapable, while his secretary rushed to his side to take the dark suit jacket he was in the process of shedding.

'Lisa, did you get my message regarding Cassandra?' he asked, while at the same time loosening his tie and undoing the top button of his shirt.

Lisa Hampton frowned and shook her head, her hitherto perfect composure slipping slightly.

'There's a note somewhere on your desk,' he muttered, his attention on the shirt-sleeves he was rolling up profusely haired, deeply tanned arms. 'Cassandra's joining the management team—she'll be sorting out the Tower.' His eyes caught Cassandra's, an edge of mockery in their amusement before he welcomed her with a smile of stunning brilliance. 'And she's to have total access to me—understood?'

For a split second Cassandra was convinced Lisa's darkly lipsticked mouth was about to gape open with shock, then she experienced a twinge of envy at the skill with which the girl so quickly regained her composure.

'I'll see that Personnel get her details immediately—and, of course, Security.'

'The security aspect has already been dealt with,' stated Sacha, and added, a trifle unkindly, Cassandra felt, 'which accounts for her not being stranded in the lobby right now.' He turned to his newest employee. 'Come along, Cassandra, there's no time like the present.' He strode towards his office, calling over his shoulder as he opened the door, 'Lisa, see if you can get the Tower mail up to us on the double, will you?'

The first week had been a nightmare, and the second little better, Cassandra admitted with candid resignation. Though there had been moments of respite—those times when she was left to her own devices in the tranquillity of the Tower, with only the toing and froing academics going about their unhurried business, and the handful of permanent staff, so comfortable and approachable compared to the calculated indifference of those she had come across in the rest of the company.

But it was working so closely with Sacha Carmichael that was stretching her nerves to fraying-point, despite its having only taken a couple of days for her to realise the intuitive wisdom in his having employed her.

And it was a job she would have considered well-nigh perfect, had it not been for the volatile human dynamo with whom it threw her into such stifling closeness. But the trouble was that the more it sank in just how much this work meant to her, both in financial and in job satisfaction terms, the more edgy and less confident she became—terrified she would do something that would make her lose it.

It had reached a stage when she had begun losing sleep over the explosive exchanges she and Sacha invariably had whenever he failed to concur with a request she considered important. So she had begun making a concerted effort to be more diplomatic in her dealings with him—unsuccessfully, she had to admit, when her attempts at diplomacy had seemed only to incense him.

The inevitable showdown came towards the end of her third week, and it came on a day when, despite the good news she had for him, Cassandra was feeling particularly vulnerable. Reading between the lines of the letter she had received from Helen that morning had led her to suspect what might lie behind her sister's secret despair.

Murmuring a greeting to the still coolly reserved receptionist, she resolutely cast aside her troubled thoughts and entered Sacha's office for what had become their regular morning meeting. She would deal with other matters before giving him the good news, she decided, closing the door behind her and acknowledging the hand he raised in absent-minded greeting while he continued to talk into a phone.

Cassandra drew up a chair and placed an open file in front of him.

'What's this?' he demanded, replacing the receiver while his eyes quickly scanned the top page of the open file.

'It's Jill Ward's file—the girl who's been working as my general factotum,' she replied, masking an irritation brought about by the fact that she now knew him well enough to know that his initial brief glance had told him exactly what file it was.

Saying nothing, he turned to face her, allowing his eyes to do his questioning for him—another habit of his she found both patronising and irritating.

'It's just that she's employed as a secretary and I think it only fair that she should be upgraded to personal assistant...her work most certainly merits it.' An understatement if ever she had heard one, she told herself, because Jill's patient and willing assistance had been a godsend to her.

'Cassandra, if I was to ask you to define the specific differences between the role of secretary and that of assistant, would you be able to do so?'

She felt her teeth clench as she bit back an angry retort. Why on earth couldn't he—just this once—agree to what she asked without subjecting her to one of his interminable lectures on company procedure?

'All I can say is that Jill——' She broke off as the phone rang and he lifted the receiver and barked out his name.

'Deborah, my darling,' he drawled with a distinct lack of warmth, tilting his body back in the large swivel chair.

Cassandra got to her feet to leave, only to be prevented by the hand that whipped out and caught her by the wrist.

'Hang on a moment, will you, Deborah?' He glanced up at Cassandra, letting go of her. 'Stay right where you are, this won't take a moment.'

She sat down again, wondering how his darling Deborah would react to learning how brief their chat would be—he hadn't even bothered to place his hand over the mouthpiece. And it gradually occurred to her that, no matter where she had been sitting, it still would have been impossible not to detect the cold rage gradually entering his tone, nor the deliberate insult he was injecting into his frequent use of endearments.

'When I whisper sweet nothings, that's exactly what they are—nothing. Perhaps you should have a word with my solicitor and see if he can put it any plainer,' he snapped, then slammed down the receiver.

Cassandra rose to her feet once more. 'Perhaps I should come back later,' she muttered uncomfortably.

'Why—because poor Sacha's just had words with his lady love?' he drawled, rising and towering intimidatingly over her. 'Cassandra, will you for God's sake stop pussyfooting around me—can't you see it's like a red rag to a bull?'

Feeling confused and apprehensive, she took a reflex couple of steps back from him. 'It's obvious you're upset——'

'Damn it, Cassandra!' he exploded, catching her by the shoulders and shaking her impatiently. 'The only thing that's upsetting me is——' He let out a bellow of rage as she kicked him hard on his left shin in her panicking attempts to free herself.

'Mr Carmichael, are you all right?' exclaimed an agitated Lisa, bursting into the room.

'I'm perfectly all right,' he scowled, limping back to his seat and waving an impatiently dismissive hand in her direction.

Her heart in her mouth, Cassandra watched as he gingerly rolled up his trouser leg and began inspecting his shin.

'Is it bad?' she whispered, unable to think of anything else to say.

'You managed to stop short of actually drawing blood,' he informed her with acerbity, 'but only just.'

Her mouth sandpaper-dry, Cassandra began uttering the words now forming in her mind. 'I suppose this is an appropriate time to tell you that yesterday I managed to crack the codes and gained access to the missing computer files.'

He broke off from his cautious inspection of his shin to gaze up at her with a look of amused incredulity.

She ignored both his look and the nervously churning sensation in the pit of her stomach. 'I'll make sure Jill is thoroughly familiar with the entire system before I go——'

'Go?' he demanded sharply. 'Where are you off to?'

'I think it's perfectly clear to both of us that I can't remain here,' she stated expressionlessly. 'And anyway, now that you've access to the administration files, your main problem's been solved—I can hardly be described as indispensable.'

'For heaven's sake, Cassandra, haven't you learned *anything* in these weeks here?' he exclaimed exasperatedly. 'Who knew, apparently off the top of her head, who to contact when the proofs of those Sanskrit translations suddenly appeared from the blue? Who instinctively knew that Professor Heyer must have been the man my father would have had lined up for...hell, what's the point?' He broke off angrily, leaping to his feet and going over to the coffee percolator in a corner of the room and switching it on.

Suddenly he swung round, ramming his hands into his pockets as he leaned back against the wall and fixed his gaze on her.

'I had a feeling something had to give sooner or later, which was why I planned having a word with you today—to see what could be done about sorting out our working relationship.' He paused, his eyes suddenly narrowing.

'Perhaps I'd have been wasting my breath…perhaps you really don't want the job after all.'

'Of course I want it!' she blurted out vehemently before she could stop herself. 'But——'

'Good—so at least this grovelling I'm doing to try to get you to stay stands a chance of succeeding.'

Cassandra blinked in astonishment, while the unlikely image his words created in her mind brought an unconscious smile to her lips.

As though that fleeting smile had been precisely the signal he was awaiting, he pounced. 'So why don't we just discuss this in a civilised manner over a cup of coffee?' he murmured. 'Do you take milk and sugar?'

'Just milk,' she replied, bemused yet fascinated. In the past, whenever he had wanted coffee, he had either got her to make it for him—or bellowed for Lisa.

He brought two cups over to the desk. 'One thing that intrigues me is how you managed to crack my father's coding system. I've a couple of friends who've been working on it for weeks now—purely as an intellectual exercise—and I've a feeling they're going to be most put out to hear you've beaten them to it.'

'Perhaps I had an unfair advantage over them in that I had all your father's non-confidential codes as a base from which to start,' she began warily, her mind having considerable difficulty adjusting to his sudden switch of mood.

'So had they.'

'The real key was your father's rather delightful sense of humour,' she told him, her tone still wary. 'Though it would probably take an age to explain why.'

'You're completely right about his sense of humour,' he remarked, his eyes never once leaving her as he paused to take a drink. 'And another thing about him was that, despite his dedication to the Tower and despite its being his sanctuary when my mother first died, he never for one moment renounced the outside world—unlike you, Cassandra,' he continued softly. 'You don't seem to have much success in your sorties out of your own private tower, especially not when you try conforming to that world beyond its environs.'

'I don't really know what you mean,' she said, squirming.

'Don't you?' he asked. 'You once told me that blunt speaking was the only method of communication you were really at home with—and I admired you for it... Oh, yes,' he assured her as he caught her startled expression of disbelief, 'I most certainly admired it...which is why I find it all the more infuriating when you start pussyfooting around me like all the rest of them. Cassandra, if there's one thing I can't stand it's people trying to "handle" me—especially women, who unfortunately often seem hell-bent on it as though driven by vocation. And most especially not you, not only because I have the feeling it goes completely against your nature, but also because you're so incredibly bad at it.'

'I had to try something,' she protested weakly. 'We always ended up having such arguments.'

'And your hamfisted attempts at diplomacy resulted in our billing and cooing, did they?' he drawled.

'Of course not!' she exclaimed.

'Cassandra, the only reason I appear to quibble every time you come up with a decision is that I'm trying to get you to see things in the context of the entire company, not just from within the narrow parameters of the Tower...and besides, I'd begun to enjoy the novelty of you coming at me with both barrels blazing.'

'But I thought...' she began, her words petering away to a bemused silence as she tried to work out exactly what it was she had thought—apart from fearing her job was in jeopardy.

'For heaven's sake, Cassandra, you couldn't possibly have thought I'd fire you, or anything as ludicrous as that, just because you spoke your mind!'

She kept her eyes resolutely on the cup before her, certain they would betray her.

'My God...you actually did,' he groaned, shaking his head in disbelief.

'Simple common sense told me that having shouting matches with my employer could hardly be regarded as normal business practice,' she protested defensively. 'I know it's no excuse, but I just don't know how people behave—are expected to behave in work relationships...I honestly haven't any idea!'

'Your coffee's cold,' he stated brusquely. 'I'll get you another.'

'Why?' she demanded, her pent-up frustration spilling over. 'You've never bothered about getting me coffee before. And now you're practically pouring cup after cup down my throat!'

'There's no need to exaggerate, Cassandra, I'm merely trying to handle you diplomatically,' he murmured, straight-faced. 'Pretty irritating, isn't it?'

For a second she looked at him with total disbelief. Then she burst out laughing.

'That's much better,' he grinned, picking up both their cups, 'and, just to prove how fair-minded I am, I'll let you get the next lot—OK?'

But there was no trace of humour on his face when he returned with their refilled cups; his look was one of deep contemplation.

'Cassandra, I'm not given to delving into the personal histories of my employees, but I get the feeling that it's only understanding what it is that makes you tick that will make it possible for me to understand how you could have been so completely unaware of the invaluable job you've been doing. And one, I sincerely hope, you'll continue to be involved in right up until the day the Alcaeus manuscripts lay claim to you.'

'That long?' croaked Cassandra, relief flooding her.

'That long,' he chuckled. 'In fact, several months of no-holds-barred combat between us until that day.' He took a sip from his cup, his eyes shrewdly watchful. 'But I was serious about needing to know what makes you tick,' he added quietly. 'Tell me about yourself... for instance, do you have brothers and sisters?'

'Just one sister—Helen.' The memory of that morning's letter flared up in her mind before she hastily suppressed it. 'She's four years older than I am, and she lectures in mathematics at Boston University.'

'So your big sister is far away in America,' he mused. 'And your mother?'

'She died just before I was three.' Led by the probing insistence of his questioning, she explained how she and Helen had spent virtually their entire lives in the rarefied atmosphere of academe.

'It must have played havoc with your schooling, swanning back and forth between Harvard and Cambridge like that with your father,' he commented. 'The British and American education systems must be poles apart.'

'I've obviously not explained clearly—Helen and I have never been inside an ordinary school in our lives.' As she continued speaking, she began to realise just how odd it must sound to an outsider to hear of two girls being privately tutored, from earliest childhood, by a handful of some of the finest minds in the academic world.

'Perhaps it was a novelty to them to begin with,' she reflected aloud. 'But they've all since admitted it was an opportunity none of them could resist—being given *carte blanche* to educate two young minds from kindergarten right up to post-graduate level.'

'It sounds rather more like a ghastly experiment to me,' observed Sacha quietly.

'Why ghastly?' asked Cassandra, surprised. 'Unique, admittedly—there can't be many people around who can claim to have had Professor Rolf Zimmerman of Harvard as a maths tutor since the age of four. But sad too—in that they showed up the inadequacies in the education systems on both sides of the Atlantic.'

He flashed her a puzzled look.

'Because the inescapable truth is that neither Helen nor I are any more intelligent than the average university student, yet, when it came to sitting our degrees, unlike the average student we could have taken ours in any one of a dozen subjects, and in the ones we chose we both achieved first-class honours.'

'Yet something tells me there's another side to this rosy picture, Cassandra,' he stated quietly.

And of course he was right, she admitted silently to herself, hesitating as she searched for suitably neutral words. To a man, their eminent tutors had encouraged their young pupils to question; to use their burgeoning knowledge to argue a point. And, to a man, they had beamed their satisfaction when those young minds had learned to pounce on their deliberately introduced errors, tearing them to shreds with self-confident delight.

'Unfortunately that doesn't seem to be the way things are done in general education,' she sighed. When Helen had, out of the blue, enrolled in a course at a local technical college at the age of seventeen, she had left before the end of the first week, bruised and disillusioned by the experience. 'You see, when the lecturer made a mistake, which unfortunately he did frequently, Helen had automatically picked him up on it...except, of course, that this particular lecturer wasn't playing any game. And her experiences with her fellow students were little better; I suppose they'd just never come across anyone like Helen before and so they just dismissed her as weird.'

'But you'd spent all your lives on one campus of another,' protested Sacha. 'Surely you were used to mixing?'

'We often attended lectures as we got older, but...I don't know...perhaps it was just that we were Professor Lestor's daughters and on first-name terms, from when we were tiny, with those the students held in awe.'

She fell into a brooding silence, conscious that she was approaching dangerous ground. When Helen had advised strongly against any mention of the debt they were in to Sacha, she had immediately seen the wisdom of such advice. But it was another area altogether that now troubled her and which a deep-seated loyalty to her father prevented her from entering. Even now she felt herself cringe at the memory of the subtle intellectual put-downs to which her father had subjected those male students with whom Helen had formed friendships. Few had had the courage to accept a second invitation to Professor Lestor's home—and only one a third. Charles Maynard, a handsome and entertainingly articulate medical student, had suffered that exquisitely delicate mind-probing ordeal on three occasions. But even Charles had not returned a fourth time, and the realisation that her then nineteen-year-old sister had grown to love him had deeply troubled Cassandra. And it troubled her now, perhaps even more deeply, to know that Charles was once again in Helen's life, because she feared it was his presence that was the cause of her sister's despair.

'I'm afraid I seem to have stirred up something of a mental hornets' nest for you—I'm sorry,' said Sacha, perception rather than sympathy in his words as they cut across the silence created by her brooding thoughts. 'Somehow I get the impression that your father has quite a lot to answer for,' he added in that same observant tone.

'He did what he believed to be best by us,' pointed out Cassandra, her own tone slightly defensive. 'And I think he was very proud of us.'

'And perhaps, in some ways, he had a right to be,' he conceded. 'I don't know about your sister, but at least you appear noticeably different from the general run of women.'

'In what way?' she asked cautiously.

'You come over as being neither predatory nor materialistic, though I dare say there's plenty of time yet for you to develop both those feminine characteristics.'

'Good heavens, you really don't like women, do you?' she exclaimed, thrown by the casual venom behind his words.

'No, I can't say that I do particularly,' he admitted, unabashed. 'Though I'd hate there to be any misunderstanding—I'm a perfectly normal red-blooded male... Cassandra, your father did warn you about us red-blooded males, didn't he?' he added mockingly.

'Yes, he did,' she retorted, humiliation brought about by the hot colour she could feel on her cheeks goading her into adding, 'Helen and I always had complete freedom regarding our relationships with men—so they hold no mysteries for us.' Complete freedom to have virtually no relationships whatever with men, argued a shocked inner voice accusingly.

'I'm afraid you'll have to forgive my negative attitude,' he murmured with no discernible regret. 'But it's one of your species who happens to be suing me at the moment for breach of contract—the fact that there was no contract between us for me to breach being a technicality she refuses to consider. And it's yet another who's lured my kid brother Max into her scheming clutches... It seems there's nothing most women find more appetising than a really wealthy man, especially, as in my brother's case, a malleable young one half her age.'

'What—your brother's married a woman twice his age?' asked Cassandra, fascinated. 'How old is he?'

'He's twenty-two, nine years younger than I am, and no, he hasn't married her, but he soon damned well will if she gets her way.'

'Is she very beautiful? You know, at forty-four some women look stunningly good——'

'I've no idea what she looks like, never having met her,' he cut in impatiently. 'And by twice his age I didn't mean it quite as literally as you appear to have taken it—whatever her exact age, it's a darned sight more than his.'

'If you haven't met her, how on earth can you be so sure she's after his money?' protested Cassandra. 'They could just be in love with one another.'

'Don't be so damned naïve! What else would you suggest a mature woman could see in a man of his age?'

'It could be his personality,' she retorted. 'Or even his looks.'

'Personality, my foot!' he exclaimed witheringly. 'Though I'll grant you most women are suckers for good looks—but when it really comes to the crunch it's the money that pulls them every time.'

'With an attitude like that, it seems no more than poetic justice to me that a woman's suing you for some of your precious money,' she flung at him in disgust.

For an instant there was a charged silence between them.

'Is that so?' he responded at last, his words so peculiarly strangled that her outrage became diluted by alarm.

He rose to his feet, startling her by taking hold of her by the arms and drawing her upright. It was then that it dawned on her he was laughing.

'Oh dear, perhaps I haven't learned much about what makes you tick...but at least I'm not being subjected to your diplomacy any more.' He smiled that lazy, stunningly transforming smile of his that she had seen so seldom she had never really had an opportunity to analyse what it was she found so extraordinary about it. 'Nothing but plain speaking between us from now on—agreed?'

She nodded, her mind a little preoccupied with puzzling over why she had begun wishing he wasn't smiling. Then she felt his hand cup and lift her chin, and suddenly her wish had come true, he was no longer smiling. She heard the soft rasp of her own intake of breath as she became aware of the sudden watchful stillness in him.

'Cassandra,' he whispered huskily, his hands tightening painfully on her arms as his eyes widened a fraction before becoming filled with a luminous darkness. Then, with the same disconcerting suddenness he had taken hold of her, he released her, gathering up the file from his desk and placing it in her unresponsive hands. 'Here, take this and leave me whatever you have on the administration files...you have brought me something, haven't you?'

It was when she felt the file he had handed her begin to slip from her numb hands that Cassandra gave a small start and experienced a sensation she could only describe as being like coming out of a trance. Feeling shaken, yet still peculiarly detached, she retrieved the file she had prepared for him from the floor beside her chair and handed it to him.

'I suggest you go and tell Jill the good news—about her promotion,' he stated, adding emphasis to his pointed termination of the meeting by picking up a phone and dialling a number.

CHAPTER THREE

WITH Jill's file clutched against her like a shield, Cassandra made her way back to the Tower. There was a look of pensive brooding on her face as she wondered exactly how much of what had inexplicably flared between them had registered with Sacha. More to the point, exactly how much of her own incomprehensible reaction to that swift and ruthlessly suppressed flash of naked desire that had burned momentarily in his eyes. No matter what her almost total inexperience with men, there could be no mistaking what she had witnessed. And neither could there be any mistaking the staggeringly powerful surge of excitement that had coursed through her, triggered solely by that momentary fire in his eyes.

She supposed she should be a little offended by the ease with which he had recovered his composure, but gave wry thanks that she was blessed with a mite more sense than that. She had had enough trouble with her two tentative sorties into the realms of romance not to have learned a lesson. And neither of those men had been anything approaching the sophisticated man of the world Sacha undoubtedly was ... just as neither of them had stirred feelings in her remotely resembling what that one brief and unguarded look from Sacha had.

Rolling her eyes in exasperation at the faint fluttering her thoughts had started up in her stomach, she pushed open the door and entered Jill Ward's office.

'You're back early.' Jill smiled, looking up from her work and removing a sheet from the typewriter. 'Was our lord and master thrilled to bits with the news?'

'He was still doing cartwheels round his office as I left,' said Cassandra with a grin, relieved to find her stomach returned to normal as she took a seat and glanced affectionately across at the smiling, auburn-haired girl.

'Well, so he should be,' exclaimed Jill. 'I hope he realises what a mountain of work cracking those codes has saved. Just let me finish signing these and I'll get us some coffee.'

'I'll get it,' offered Cassandra, getting to her feet. 'I suppose you don't feel like altering those——'

'Altering them!' squeaked Jill in horror. 'Cassie, it's all those letters we drafted yesterday. I've just this minute finished the last one.'

'Never mind,' laughed Cassandra. 'But you'll have to start using your new title from now on.'

'My new title?' puzzled Jill.

'Personal assistant.'

'Me?' she croaked, then gave a shriek of delight. 'Cassie, I don't believe it!'

'Why ever not, you deserve it,' chuckled Cassandra, touched by the girl's obvious pleasure. 'But I didn't dare mention it to you just in case Sacha didn't agree.'

'I can't believe he has,' exclaimed Jill. 'Oh, Cassie, thanks...thanks a million!'

'I'm the one who should be thanking you,' protested Cassandra, handing her a mug and sitting down again. 'If it hadn't been for you, I honestly wouldn't have known where to begin here.'

'Precisely my feelings the day I walked in here as a raw temp,' sighed Jill. 'Which is why I was only too

happy to share with you what little I'd ferreted out...
Which reminds me,' she added, her eyes twinkling, 'I
was talking to one of the girls in main office Personnel
yesterday—it's probably eighty per cent gossip, but it
does shed a little light on why the Tower was suddenly
left without any administrative staff.'

'You mean Mrs Jessel's sudden retirement,' said
Cassandra.

Jill shook her head. 'I always thought the time factor
was a bit odd considering when Mrs Jessel actually retired, and I was right. You see, the section actually did
carry on after she had gone—in the hands of her very
competent secretary.' She flashed Cassandra an impish
grin. 'Well, competent as far as work went, but it seems
she made the fatal error of falling hook, line and sinker
for the gorgeous Sacha.'

'Not the most intelligent of moves,' murmured
Cassandra. But a folly she found a shade easier to
understand today than she might have yesterday, she realised with a pang of unease.

'It also seems that he wasn't averse to a little mixing
of business with pleasure... for a while. It was when he
eventually lost interest that the Tower, virtually over-
night, I gather, lost the last person familiar with its administrative procedures.'

Cassandra's eyes were wide with shocked disbelief.
'You mean she actually had access to the computer files—
to everything—and deliberately left no information for
her successor?'

Jill nodded. 'As they say—hell hath no fury like a
woman scorned,' she sighed. 'And, on reflection, I have
to admit that when I arrived on the scene Sacha did seem
to be having considerable difficulty in accepting the

extent of the information he was unable to gain access to.'

'No wonder he's so determined to have at hand every detail imaginable connected with the running of the section,' mused Cassandra, noting how much truer this version of his difficulties rang than the sanitised one Sacha had given her. She glanced across at Jill and grinned. 'She certainly managed to hit him where it hurt, didn't she?'

'I suppose with his looks and money he's bound to come in for more than his fair share of female attention,' chuckled Jill. 'But his lack of finesse in getting rid of them does seem to backfire disastrously. First the one here—and now some other woman, claiming to be his fiancée, suing him for breach of contract.' She laughed at Cassandra's startled look, completely misinterpreting it. 'It's something I came across in a gossip column in yesterday's paper.'

'Talking of gossip—it's something we really haven't time to be indulging in right now,' sighed Cassandra, glancing at her watch and rising. 'Apart from a pile of other things, I haven't even gone through this morning's post yet. I trust there's nothing earth-shattering in it?'

Jill shook her head as Cassandra opened the door of her own adjoining office. 'Though there's an invitation to something called the Whittaker Awards—perhaps the Tower's in the running for an Oscar or something!'

'Damn it, Cassandra, these Whittaker Awards are to-night—why on earth didn't you bring this to my attention earlier?' exclaimed Sacha the next morning, glowering down at the engraved invitation before him.

'Because it only arrived yesterday,' replied Cassandra. 'Perhaps it got held up in the post... Is it terribly important?'

'My father was very friendly with old Whittaker and always made a point of attending these Awards.'

'So now you can go in his stead.'

'I already have something on this evening,' he snapped. 'But I'll just have to get out of it. Did you ring up and accept the invitation when it arrived?'

Cassandra's face fell; it was something that hadn't even occurred to her.

With an exclamation of impatience he buzzed through to Lisa on the intercom. 'Lisa, could you get on to someone at the Whittaker Foundation at once and let them know Cassandra and I will be attending the Awards tonight... thanks.'

Cassandra, who had been casually reading the invitation as he was speaking, let out a squeak of protest. 'What do you mean—me?' she demanded in consternation. 'Why on earth should I go?'

'Because you, technically, happen to head the section to which the invitation was issued,' he informed her coldly.

'But you never mentioned anything about... about my ever having to attend social functions.'

'I didn't have to—it's all there in the contract you signed.'

Cassandra swallowed hard. 'Well, I'm not going,' she stated flatly. 'The least you could have done was warn me about things like this... and besides, it's formal, and I've nothing even remotely suitable to wear.' She gave an inward groan of disbelief as those ingenuous words tripped lightly off her tongue—why couldn't she for once in her life come up with a spontaneous, preferably watertight lie? 'Sacha, I'm just not going,' she reiterated stubbornly as he treated her to a particularly withering look.

'Oh yes you are. And we'll just have to get you something suitable to wear—now!'

Grasping her by the arm, he hauled her to her feet and dragged her, protesting vociferously, to the door, where they almost collided with Lisa, her hand still raised to knock and who now gazed at them both with open-mouthed amazement.

'Did you get through to Whittaker's?' demanded Sacha, keeping a firm hold on the still-furiously protesting Cassandra. 'Good,' he observed as Lisa managed to nod. 'Cassandra and I will be out for the next hour or two.'

Cassandra was still protesting when he eventually slid the gleaming white sports car in which they had travelled into a parking space near a famous London department store. But it was what she could only describe as the near-suicidal aggressiveness of his driving that was now eliciting her protests.

Though she gritted her teeth and refused to exchange a single word with him, by the time he had hauled her into the unfamiliar luxury of the store's designer rooms she had just about resigned herself to the fact that this was a battle she had little chance of winning.

'And what sort of gown had madam in mind?' enquired the fashion-plate of a saleswoman once Sacha had vaguely stated their requirements.

'Madam had nothing in mind,' snapped Cassandra, wishing she hadn't as she inwardly winced at the sound of her own churlish rudeness.

As though adhering to an utterly commonplace routine, it was Sacha the woman led to a row of gowns, leaving Cassandra alone in the centre of acres of cream-carpeted elegance and feeling for all the world like an ill-mannered brat being thoroughly snubbed.

And for all she knew this *was* a commonplace routine for Sacha, she thought disparagingly, irritated that she was unable to hear what was being said as they glanced several times in her direction. Perhaps he brought his women here by the drove, imperiously selecting clothing for them like some omnipotent feudal lord.

Eventually five dresses were selected, and, by the time she had tried on and been forced to parade in all five before two pairs of critical eyes, she was feeling like an exhibit in a cattle market.

'It fits, doesn't it?' she exploded, as Sacha imperiously rejected the fifth dress—just as he had the preceding four.

'And that's about all it does,' he snapped as she flounced past him and back to the changing-room.

Well, that was that little problem solved, Cassandra told herself triumphantly as she slipped back into her own clothes. Cinderella would not, after all, be dragged off to the ball!

'The gentleman would like you to try this,' murmured the saleswoman, popping her head round the door and handing Cassandra yet another dress. 'This one really is rather special,' she coaxed as she saw Cassandra's face fall.

With a sigh of resignation, Cassandra examined the dress. It was in a deep midnight-blue, its material like silken gossamer to the touch.

She slipped it on, then cursed in exasperation as she saw her reflection—the dress was strapless and she still had on her bra. But it certainly was a beautiful dress, the first of any she had tried on that had appealed to her in the least. And this one appealed very much, she realised, surprised to feel a small thrill of pleasure as she studied her reflection.

Of course, the bra was all wrong, she thought, chuckling at its stark white incongruity against the rich blue. She had just given in to the fact that she had no option but to remove it when she spotted the matching stole draped over the hanger. Grabbing the stole, she drew it round her shoulders, then carefully eased the bra from sight.

'This one's OK—and it fits,' she announced, walking towards her critics. She gave one quick twirl, then started back for the changing-room.

'Cassandra!' bellowed Sacha after her retreating back.

She turned resignedly, to find him striding towards her with a face like a thundercloud.

'How can I possibly see what the bloody thing looks like when you're muffled up to your eyeballs in this?' he demanded, whipping the stole from around her and exposing the bra in most of its glory.

With a softly muttered oath, he spun her round. For a fleeting moment there was the sensation of deft fingers against her back, then he slipped the bra off her arms and rammed it into his jacket pocket.

'Turn round—right round,' he ordered, reducing her to speechless rage as his eyes coolly raked the length of her body. 'That's fine—or it would be if you closed your mouth and stopped gawping like an indignant goldfish.'

He then turned to the assistant, his smile angelic as he told her they would take the dress.

'Cassandra!' he called after her as she stalked away.

'Now what do you want?' she almost shrieked.

'Won't you be needing this?' He drew her bra from his pocket and tossed it over to her.

But, true to her own irrepressible sense of humour, she was having difficulty choking back laughter by the time she reached the changing-room. It really had served her right for not removing the bra, she had to admit, chuckling as she remembered the look on the saleswoman's face when Sacha had removed the stole.

And it really was a fairy-tale of a dress, she thought dreamily, drawing it up over her head. So soft and silky... She gave a sharp yelp of pain as the object of her reveries became caught in her hair and refused her frantic efforts to dislodge it.

'I'm stuck!' she wailed as she heard the door open.

'What the hell are you doing?' demanded Sacha's exasperated voice.

'I think the zip's caught in my hair.'

'Cassandra, for heaven's sake stop tugging at it like that—you'll have the whole thing in shreds!'

She felt his fingers at the back of her neck, their touch unexpectedly delicate as they painstakingly extricated her.

'Thank heavens for that!' she exclaimed, heaving a sigh of relief as he drew the freed dress off over her head. 'I always seem to be getting my hair caught in...' She stopped suddenly, her senses sledge-hammering her mind into awareness of the slightly abrasive sensation of the material of his jacket against her naked breasts.

Her name was no more than a whispered groan on his lips as his arms encircled her and his mouth found hers.

She felt the sharp savage jolt of her first true encounter with desire as her body trembled beneath hands that moved in urgent caress against its nakedness while her lips yielded to those parting them in swift, demanding hunger.

Yet even as that mindless turbulence of excitement threatened to possess her completely, there was that minute part of her standing back, desperate in its attempts to remain dissociated from the abandoned welcome by her body of the unfamiliar delights bombarding it. And it was that tiny, still sane part of her that experienced fear when her passion-drugged senses began responding with blatantly physical spontaneity to the inflammatory signals of desire emanating from the taut masculine body against hers.

And, as fear and passion swelled in fierce conflict within her till one was no longer distinguishable from the other, her panicking body declared its unreasoned war on both. It was only when her teeth had bitten, half in fear, half in the savagery of an insatiable need, against the moist fullness of his lower lip, and only when he had flung her from him with a sharp oath of outrage, that her madness began to dissipate.

While she strove to gain control over the ragged harshness of her breathing, she found herself witnessing the last vestiges of astonishment turn to fury in his eyes and then the crimson spot of blood on the handkerchief he had raised to his mouth.

'Dress yourself,' he ordered abruptly, picking up the dress and striding from the cubicle.

Slumping weakly against the smooth coolness of the wall, Cassandra closed her eyes and tried to will the terrible shaking racking her to cease. Then she slowly began dressing, and only when she had completely finished did she turn and face herself in the mirrored wall.

Barely conscious of her actions, she traced the outline of her mouth, seeing and feeling the bruised aftermath of its passionate encounter. Her hand froze as she was suddenly reliving in every detail of its savage force the havoc those other lips had wrought on hers.

She leaned her burning forehead against the contrasting cold of the mirror, emitting a soft sigh of hopeless frustration as the only immediate solution presenting itself to her was the hope that the ground might open up and swallow her.

She should have heeded the warning signs, of which there had been plenty; from that uncomfortable feeling of empathy she had experienced towards the woman Sacha had snubbed that very first time she had seen him, to the rumours about Jill's predecessor, and most of all her own disturbing reaction that time to the mere sight of desire flaming momentarily in his eyes. But she had heeded nothing, and when, like the red-blooded male he made no bones about being, he had responded with complete predictability to the presence of a virtually naked woman in his arms, she had behaved in a manner that now both appalled and frightened her.

She straightened with an audible groan as another unpalatable thought struck her. Not long ago she had bemoaned her inability to come up with a spontaneous lie—but now she was remembering that occasion when she had claimed to have always had complete freedom and ease in her relationships with men. She could hardly do an about-turn now, she reasoned dejectedly, and admit that her violent panic had been caused largely by total inexperience.

To hell with it all, she thought, with a valour born of complete desperation, and marched out to meet her fate head-on: the way her life was going at the moment, this latest development could only be considered par for the course!

It was in the company of a tight-lipped and icy stranger that she left the store, the box containing the dress clutched bulkily against her as she rushed to keep pace with his impatient stride. And it was not until they were both seated in the car that he chose to break the heavily charged silence between them.

'You can't imagine what comfort I derive from knowing I don't have to bother mincing words with you,' he began, twisting round to face her. 'So we'll just cut out the games and get right down to business.'

'I beg your pardon?' she croaked inanely, her tenuous valour deserting her in the face of those sententious and, to her, completely unintelligible words.

'Cassandra, I said we'd dispense with the games,' he warned with chilling softness, his hand reaching out to rest lightly against the side of her neck, his thumb searching momentarily, then moving almost caressingly against the erratically throbbing pulse its search had located.

Not daring to move, Cassandra opened her mouth to protest, quickly snapping it shut when words failed to come.

'I can't honestly say that playing rough has ever really held much attraction for me,' he murmured, the chilling smile accompanying his words, and on which Cassandra's almost mesmerised gaze had become unwillingly fixed, seeming to accentuate that small telltale area of swollen darkness on his lower lip. 'But, if that's the way you want it, I'm prepared to go along... always within reason, of course.'

He was talking gibberish and was doing so both to punish and to rattle her, she told herself with a good deal of irritation and rather less of conviction... There was no other explanation she could think of.

'Of course, it's only fair that there should be a bit of give and take on both sides...don't you agree, Cassandra?' He paused, his questioning look receiving an answer of glowering irritation. 'You really don't like having your bluff called, do you?' he observed with a soft chuckle of satisfaction. 'Anyway, where was I? Ah, yes...give and take.'

He really was enjoying himself! thought Cassandra furiously, allowing her eyes another quick inspection of the damage her teeth had wrought on his mouth and experiencing, much to her comfort, a positive thrill of satisfaction rather than any remorse.

'Cassandra, you'll really have to do something about your appearance. Your hair is a mess, you use nothing in the way of make-up and you dress appallingly.'

This was more like it, she thought with relief, perfectly intelligible insults flowing fast and furious.

'You omitted to mention my thick skin,' she retorted sweetly. 'Which reduces your insults to no more than a waste of your breath.'

'Cassandra, you misjudge me,' he responded, just as sweetly, his hand now slipping round to the back of her neck where his fingers began toying idly in her hair. 'It wasn't my intention to insult you, it's just that there are certain aesthetic standards I require in my women, and at the moment you meet few, if any of them.'

While he had been speaking, Cassandra had been devoting much of her attention to wrestling with the serious problem created by the fact that the casual movement of his fingers against her neck was sending disturbingly powerful ripples of pleasure racing up and down her spine. There was a consequent delay before any of his words—and most particularly 'my women'—penetrated her mind and started the alarm bells jangling in it.

'So, to get back to the question of your appearance——'

'*Your* women!' she shrieked. 'You can't honestly, seriously believe I'd ever in a million years want to join your harem!'

He said nothing, and neither did his expression register anything. He merely reached out unhurriedly, took her by the shoulders and drew her against him. And there was neither anger nor impatience in the mouth that leisurely covered hers.

Her reaction was one of dumbstruck outrage. Yet even though her body tensed and twisted in response to that outrage, and even though her lips clamped tightly shut in implacable denial, there was never any roughness in the hands that stilled her, nor any hint of force in the mouth that coaxed inexorably against hers. In fact, it was the unexpected gentleness of those determinedly questing lips that ultimately parted hers, and it was their leisurely sensuality that sparked an insatiable flame in her, stilling her body to voluptuous acquiescence and bringing up her arms to cling around his neck in an unconscious gesture of total surrender.

When he later drew his mouth from hers and gazed down at her from eyes softened by the darkness of desire, there was the hoarse catch of need in his voice when he spoke.

'Kiss me, Cassandra.'

And she drew down his head to hers once more, the trembling urgency of a longing more powerful than any she had before experienced betraying itself in the reckless ardency with which she obeyed his demand.

His hands moved compulsively against her, a stifled groan escaping him as his lips outstripped the guileless abandon of those offered and began their own ruthless, far more explicitly demanding plunder. And this time, when he eventually drew back from her, the response she gave was a sharp, undisguised cry of protest. But this time, when he drew back, it was to disengage himself completely from the clinging softness of her arms.

And it was in a sickened, frozen silence that she watched him get the keys from his jacket pocket, watched as his lean fingers separated one to insert in the ignition, while at the same time wondering how she could possibly have lived all these years in total ignorance of the terrible flaw in her that would one day rise up and take possession of her, negating her mind and rendering her a slave to the caress of a man as calculatingly manipulative as this man beside her.

He started up the car, his eyes never leaving the road ahead.

'Welcome to my harem, Cassandra,' he murmured with chilling softness, then accelerated with confident ease into the thick of the traffic.

Her eyes were tightly closed as she leaned back against the soft leather of the upholstery, blotting out the light as the darkness of her thoughts filled her mind.

Her father had always said that the inability to own up promptly and admit defeat was indicative of a seriously flawed character. She wondered what her father's reaction would have been to the deplorable defect that had just manifested itself in his younger daughter's character, and found herself giving silent thanks that it was something she would never know.

CHAPTER FOUR

DURING the hours following Sacha's informing her that he would fetch her at eight, Cassandra had been attempting rigorous censorship of her thoughts. There had been knife-edge moments when her resolve had threatened to waver, such as the instant her hand had drawn back, as though burned, from the make-up case she kept for special occasions. It was Sacha's derogatory words about her appearance, slipping with snakelike ease into her momentarily unguarded thoughts, that had decided her that, special occasion or not, there was no way she intended doing anything to enhance her appearance. Her slight hesitation before washing her hair had been another, but she had recovered relatively quickly. Wearing no make-up was one thing, going around with unwashed hair was entirely another.

She had timed herself to be ready on the dot of eight but, thanks to her dilapidated hairdrier's having finally given up the ghost, a full ten minutes before schedule, she was sitting, damp-haired, in George Malton's splendid library, wondering if his wife, Margaret, had by any chance a spare hairdrier tucked away somewhere in the house.

Conscious that her thoughts were veering towards rebellion and open speculation as to Sacha's probable reaction to her noticeably undried hair, she began steering them along a non-contentious path—the Maltons. When George Malton had been asked to carry on her father's work in America, his one reservation had been over the idea of leaving his London home untenanted for such a long period, though he found the thought of renting it to strangers quite abhorrent. It had been his wife who had come up with the solution.

'If Cassandra really is set on living and working in London, she'll need somewhere to live—and where better than our place?'

George's relief had been so great when Cassandra had agreed that he had been adamant that not only should she live there rent-free, but that he would pay all the running costs.

'I keep my books in the best atmosphere possible,' he had claimed, 'so why should you be expected to pay for my doing so? And besides, I'll feel better knowing they have an appreciative friend to sit with them now and then.'

And, because George was an old softie she had loved since she was a child, it had become a ritual of hers to spend some time each day surrounded by his lovingly put together library. And it was thanks to George and Margaret that she could send so large a portion of her earnings to Helen, safe in the knowledge that for the next two years her only expenses would be food and clothes.

It was the thought of clothes that had her unconsciously adjusting the stole round her shoulders, but it was the ring on the doorbell that brought her to her feet in a sudden welter of panic.

She would cope with this evening because she damned well had to, a hectoring voice from within informed her as she dragged her reluctant feet towards the front door.

'I said I'd be here at eight,' said Sacha, his eyes sweeping coolly over her as she opened the door. 'You don't exactly appear ready.'

'Perhaps not, but I am,' responded Cassandra, clutching the stole around her while not altogether convincingly arguing that the demented fluttering in her stomach was caused by nothing more sinister than her keen eye for beauty... Sacha in evening dress was a sight that would stun even the most discerning female eye.

'Your hair's wet,' he pointed out with exaggerated patience.

'It isn't wet, it's just a bit damp,' she replied, her already depressed spirits plummeting further still—they would be here on the doorstep all night if he intended listing her faults one by one. 'My hairdrier packed up on me.'

The infinitesimal shrug he gave spoke volumes. 'Well, get your coat, we might as well arrive there on time.'

'I don't need a coat,' she stated, grabbing her bag and trying not to wince as she closed the door behind her and felt the sharp bite of the night air. Of course she needed a coat, but her imagination had given her a graphic picture of his likely reaction to the single one she possessed—a rather scruffy raincoat.

Not a single word passed between them during the short drive—not that Cassandra would have been capable of uttering one, with her entire concentration given up to praying that Sacha's reactions were as fast as the terrifying speed at which he drove.

'If there's anything you desperately need in that bag, I suggest you take it out and give it to me,' he told her once they were parked.

She glanced across at him in open puzzlement.

'Cassandra, that's hardly what could be described as an evening bag,' he pointed out impatiently. 'You can't possibly walk around with that thing on your arm dressed as you are.'

Gritting her teeth, but saying nothing because she realised he was right, she deposited the bulging bag on the floor and opened the car door. She was still struggling with the unaccustomed bulk of the full-length dress when he appeared at her side and put out a hand to help her.

'And while we're on the subject those shoes aren't suitable either,' he remarked, pulling her out by the hand. 'Though luckily the long skirt hides them.'

'What are you, for God's sake?' she exclaimed hotly, tearing her hand free. 'A spare-time fashion consultant?'

'Cassandra, I wouldn't push too far if I were you,' he warned softly, catching her by the arms and pulling her against him. 'There's a limit to how much I'm prepared to swallow of this hick *ingénue* routine of yours.' He gazed down at her, a mocking smile distorting his handsome features in the shadowy light. 'And besides, we both know I've found the key that unlocks the real you . . . not that we have time for me to remind you,' he added, tucking her hand through his arm and leading her into the building. 'But one thing I must remind you is that nothing can interfere with business. And as we're here in a solely business capacity we shall be presenting a united front.' As he spoke, he led her into a huge banqueting hall. 'You will therefore remove that childishly petulant look from your face and smile.'

She smiled, though as the evening wore on it was a smile she became so conscious of having to maintain that she felt her facial muscles ache from the strain.

The tables were arranged to seat groups of twelve, and it was the careless confidence of the other women, together with the almost flawless beauty of two of them, that made her rue her decision not to wear a little make-up—not, she readily admitted, that even having been professionally made up and coiffured would have made

the slightest difference to her feelings of total social in-
adequacy. But, worst of all, as the lavish meal pro-
gressed it was to Sacha she automatically turned
whenever she felt on the point of floundering, and he
was being bewilderingly supportive.

'Relax,' he murmured softly in her ear at one such
point. 'This is only dinner-table conversation. Nobody's
going to bite your head off because some of the topics
raised are unfamiliar to you.'

Gradually she relaxed enough to return the conversation of the middle-aged man to the left of her, only
to begin regretting the enthusiastic relief with which she
had done so when he began flirting with her with a heavy-
handed blatancy. In fact, she greeted with considerable
relief the sudden dimming of the lights and cessation of
all conversation when the speeches began.

'Here's where the united front really comes into play,'
whispered Sacha. 'You'll have to give me a discreet nudge
if I show signs of dropping off—this could go on
interminably.'

Which it did. At first Cassandra listened attentively,
applauding enthusiastically those receiving awards. But
gradually the smoke-laden, soporific atmosphere began
affecting her and it was all she could do to keep her eyes
from drooping—in between keeping careful watch for
similar signs in Sacha.

It was after about two hours that she felt the hand on
her thigh. Her first reaction, which she quickly suppressed, was to cry out in protest. Her second was to
turn to Sacha and tell him what her other neighbour was
up to, but as her eyes alighted on his oddly comforting
profile she was struck by a realisation she found not in
the least comforting. Had it been Sacha's hand caressing
so lightly yet insistently against her thigh, her problem

would most certainly not be the slight feeling of nausea she was now contending with.

Another, exceedingly comfortless thought then occurred to her: while she had been doing all this thinking, her neighbour's hand had been growing more confident against her leg.

She turned to face him, only to find him apparently totally engrossed in the proceedings, so she tapped him firmly on the shoulder, flinching slightly from the look on his face as he turned to her.

'If you don't remove your hand this instant,' she hissed, 'I shall tell my partner what you're doing!'

'I'd no idea I was poaching,' he said, smirking, though he had removed his hand with alacrity. 'You're not exactly what one would imagine Carmichael choosing as a replacement for the gorgeous Deborah.'

Even as she felt the flash of fury sweep through her, an inherent honesty in her was admitting that it was a response warranted more by his initial groping than his subsequent words. And she was still in the process of excusing that tardy response as delayed reaction when the raising of the lights heralded the end of the evening.

'Come on, let's get out of here,' muttered Sacha, taking the stole from the back of her chair and placing it round her shoulders.

It was extremely cold when they stepped outside, but she realised that the trembling now racking her really could, to a large extent, be put down to delayed reaction. But it was when Sacha slipped off his jacket in silence and placed it around her that it hit her with a sudden and savage force just how completely aberrant her life had become. Bizarre though it was, it had been Sacha's voice she had instinctively welcomed as that of a trusted ally when the lights had come up, and it was

Sacha's jacket now imparting the warmth of his body second-hand to hers...Sacha, her chief tormentor.

'Thank you very much for lending me your jacket,' she said, reaching up to remove it once they were seated in the car.

'No—keep it,' he muttered, switching on the engine. 'Next time perhaps you'll have enough intelligence to bring one of your own.'

Next time, she thought with a sickening dread, her hand making unconscious scrubbing movements against her left thigh. And the next and the next: the sheltered, blissfully uncomplicated existence that had once been hers was gone forever.

She glanced down at her thigh and only then became aware of the compulsive movements of her hand against it. All right, so her life had changed beyond all recognition, she remonstrated harshly with herself, and yes, she had just suffered the indignity of being groped by a despicable creep, but getting all twitchy about it wasn't going to help, and neither was wallowing in self-pity.

To help keep her mind otherwise occupied she began looking out of the car window, noting with surprise that the sights flashing past them were no longer the indistinct blur they had been on the other two occasions she had been subjected to Sacha's driving. But any comfort she derived from that observation was quickly dispelled by the imminence of the end of the journey and the fact that she had no idea what it was likely to herald.

She had her seatbelt released and her hand out ready to open the passenger door almost before he had drawn to a halt outside the house. Then she gave an audible groan of frustration as she remembered the jacket still around her and began removing it.

'For one ghastly moment I thought you were about to race off and leave me shivering here in my shirt-sleeves,' he drawled with mocking amusement. 'Why the rush, Cassandra?' he taunted, letting the jacket she had passed him fall between them as he caught hold of her wrist. 'This unflattering eagerness you're displaying to be out of my company as fast as you can...it couldn't be because you don't trust yourself alone with me, could it?'

She struggled briefly to free her hand, giving up the instant she realised the futility of such an attempt.

'Cassandra, it's pointless trying to avoid the inevitable, you know.'

It was the utter casualness of his words that knocked the wind out of her; for all the emotion he displayed he might just as easily have been forecasting rain.

'All right—I accept the inevitable,' she retorted, something in her snapping. 'One lecherous male has already whiled away his time groping me this evening, so why shouldn't another continue where he left off?'

For once she had the satisfaction of having wiped the supercilious mockery from his face.

'Jack Waddington?' he exclaimed harshly. 'You're saying that Waddington interfered with you——'

'I've no idea what his name was, I didn't catch it,' she cut in coldly. 'Perhaps a man rubbing his hand against a woman's thigh is merely one of those little social refinements I'm so ignorant about——'

'Cassandra, why the hell didn't you say something to me at the time?' he demanded, abruptly letting go of her hand.

'Because I was perfectly capable of handling him myself,' she claimed inaccurately, watching as he placed both his hands on the steering-wheel and seeing the sudden gleam of white against his knuckles from the ferocity of his grip.

'You might be perfectly capable of handling someone like Waddington,' he muttered tonelessly, suddenly releasing the steering-wheel, 'but don't forget where trying to handle me has got you.'

'At least you seem to be admitting that you and he are two of a kind,' she retorted, instantly questioning the wisdom of so reckless a response as he tensed noticeably. She felt fear stirring in the pit of her stomach as she sensed the control he was exerting over himself.

Then he picked up his jacket and threw it across her lap.

'You'd better put that on while I see you to the door—and don't forget your bag.'

Feeling thoroughly confused, cold and disconcertingly guilty at the length of time it took her to find her key in the voluminous recesses of her bag, she found herself hovering on the verge of apologising for keeping him waiting so long in the cutting wind. She was glad she had resisted when she finally located her key and he spoke.

'Cassandra, I would strongly advise you choosing your insults with more care in future,' he informed her silkily. 'Attempting to lump me together with the Waddingtons of this world was foolish and, perhaps, a little dangerous.'

'Dangerous?' she demanded, removing his jacket and handing it back to him. 'That sounds rather like a threat.'

He gave a soft laugh as he shrugged into the jacket. 'Why would I threaten you, my sweet? Especially when we both know that the day I choose to call...you'll come running only too willingly.'

*　*　*

'Sacha's been ringing you practically every five minutes demanding to know where you are,' Jill greeted her apologetically when she arrived almost half an hour late the next morning.

'That's all I need,' muttered Cassandra, slipping out of her raincoat and hanging it up. 'I got involved with a cyclist who was knocked from his bike by a passing car,' she sighed, flopping down on to a chair. 'Luckily he wasn't badly hurt, but I stayed with him till the ambulance arrived.'

'How dreadful!' exclaimed Jill sympathetically, then gave a groan as the phone rang. 'Oh, lord, that'll be Sacha again!'

Cassandra reached out and picked up the receiver.

'Cassandra, where the hell have you been?' demanded Sacha.

'I've——'

'Just get up here, will you?'

'But I haven't even——'

'Now!'

She flung the receiver back on its cradle, shaking with fury. 'God alone knows how someone as decent as Alexander Carmichael fathered a man as...as unspeakable as Sacha,' she raged.

'Cassie, I'm sure he wouldn't be getting uptight just because you're a bit late,' soothed Jill, her words not exactly overladen with conviction. 'After all, you were out late last night on business...I suppose it's pointless asking how that went?'

'Quite pointless,' muttered Cassandra wearily, then made an effort to look cheerful as she saw the anxiety on Jill's kindly face. 'You brew us a strong pot of coffee, while I go and see what's troubling the great dictator.'

He was standing before his desk with his back to her as she entered, the pale material of an expensively tailored raincoat accentuating the broadness of his shoulders. Still speaking into one of the phones, he swung round as she closed the door behind her.

'Harry, I'll call you back. Some time later today, OK?'

'Sacha——'

'Cassandra, please!' He strode to her side. 'Before you say anything—I'm sorry for the way I must have sounded. It was most rude of me.'

She glanced up at him, her astonishment written all over her face.

'Also, last night I meant to tell you to take the morning off, but it slipped my mind. And now something rather important has cropped up.'

'Oh...I see.' She didn't see in the least—her mind was still too busy reeling from the unexpectedness of his unsolicited apology.

'Look, would you mind if we got going? I'll explain on the way,' he said, taking her by the elbow and steering her back to the door. 'We'd better collect your coat.'

Back in her own offices Cassandra found herself forced to drop her eyes from Jill's when she detected an ominous twitching around the girl's mouth as Sacha solicitously helped her on with her raincoat.

Still without having offered any explanation, he rushed her down to the basement car park and into his car. She glanced across at him anxiously as he got into the driving seat; he seemed tense—almost jittery.

'Sacha, what's happened?'

'Nothing...well, nothing that should concern you. It's Mrs Jessel—I had a call from her sister this morning.'

'Is she ill?' asked Cassandra anxiously.

He shook his head, then started up the car. 'Though she was in a convalescent home for several weeks...God only knows why that damned sister of hers didn't contact me sooner!'

Cassandra waited for him to continue. So far he had made little sense, and she was finding his uncharacteristic agitation more than a little unsettling.

'The last I heard, Mildred and her sister were preparing to retire to Jersey—that's where they're from. She was to write to me once they were settled, and I simply put my not having heard from her for so long down to two old ladies taking their time getting themselves properly sorted out.'

Cassandra was momentarily distracted by a jolt of fear as they sped out into the traffic, and offered up a quick prayer that their journey would be a brief one.

'I'd intended going round to give them a hand packing up their things,' Sacha added.

His words took Cassandra by surprise.

'As luck would have it, I had to go to the States on business, though I wish to God I hadn't gone now!' he exclaimed in an explosion of self-accusation. 'Poor old Mildred managed to break a bone in her foot a few days before they were due to leave and wound up needing all that time in a convalescent home!'

Cassandra found herself looking at him in complete amazement. The stark remorse and disgust in his voice seemed to indicate a conviction that the responsibility was entirely his, yet it showed her too a side of him which, for the first time since she had known him, made it possible for her to regard him as a true son of the gentle Alexander Carmichael.

'Sacha, it's simply ridiculous for you to blame yourself,' she chided. 'The stay in the home will probably have done her a power of good before setting off for Jersey... They're still going, aren't they?'

He nodded morosely, plainly unconvinced.

'She'll think you're mad if she sees you blaming yourself like this,' she pointed out, then added, 'And I really don't understand why you're taking me along with you.'

'I just want to reassure her that the Tower's running smoothly,' he muttered, plainly not at ease. 'I'd hate to think of anything having got back to her... not that it's likely to have.'

'You don't by any chance mean word of the Tower's having been left in the lurch by her erstwhile secretary suddenly leaving, do you?' murmured Cassandra sweetly.

'It didn't take you long to find out about the delectable Melanie, did it, Cassandra?' he drawled, his tone a sharp reminder that he hadn't undergone any miraculous personality change. 'Though you're right,' he confused her by adding with a sigh. 'And if anyone's to blame for the disruption Melanie's departure caused, I am.'

'You're going to tell her the truth anyway, aren't you?' she asked intuitively.

He nodded. 'I owe it to her... and once she's spoken to you I'm sure she'll be reassured that everything's going smoothly now.'

'Sacha, I hate to be negative,' she said with resignation, 'but the idea of a rank amateur like me filling in until your father's replacement arrives might well give her heart failure!'

'I agree,' he murmured. 'You *are* being negative! The point is, you are going to see her and to answer any question she chooses to put to you. And afterwards we'll be able to judge which of us was right.'

*   *   *

'Come on, we'll find somewhere to have lunch, and you can apologise for doubting my judgement,' said Sacha as they left the elderly sisters' temporary home.

While it had cheered her to see Mrs Jessel looking so fit and so completely her normal self, Cassandra felt her spirits plummet as she realised that Sacha too was now restored to his normal self... and he had seemed almost human earlier, when racked by his unnecessary guilt and remorse.

'You go and have lunch,' she said. 'I'll catch a bus back to the office.'

He took her firmly by the elbow and led her to the car. 'Don't be such a rotten loser,' he taunted, opening the passenger door.

'I'm not,' she declared, standing her ground. 'And anyway, I didn't mean that I felt I was incapable of doing the job—just that I wasn't sure if Mrs Jessel would think I could do it.'

'OK, so I think you're capable of it, Mrs J does, and so do you, belatedly. Would you mind getting into the car? I didn't have any breakfast this morning, and I'm hungry.'

'And so am I,' replied Cassandra. 'But I also happen to know that I'll be feeling sick with fright and unable to eat a thing by the time we get to wherever it is you're going—your driving terrifies me.'

He gave her a look of complete incredulity, then threw his head back and laughed. 'I may drive fast, but I've never before been accused of driving terrifyingly!'

'Well, I happen to feel endangered when I'm in a car that misses other cars and objects by no more than a whisker.'

'They say a miss is as good as a mile—so what's your problem?' He raised his hands in a gesture of surrender as she opened her mouth to tell him precisely what her problem was. 'OK, I'll drive at ten miles an hour and give anything that comes our way the widest possible berth.'

Only because she had had actual experience of his ability to drive in a manner that didn't leave her limp with terror, she got into the car—consoling herself with the fact that she could always demand that he stop and let her out if it came to it.

Mercifully it didn't come to it, but the exaggerated slowness with which they had set off came to an end when he turned to her with a pained expression.

'Cassandra, now that I've proved to you that I'm not really the sort of man who equates his masculinity with the speed at which he drives, I feel obliged to point out that I do, nevertheless, draw the line at being overtaken by an invalid carriage—which is about to happen right now if I don't speed up a fraction!'

The restaurant to which he took her was of the dauntingly smart variety—the sort in which she had never before set foot, but which he did regularly, judging by the effusive greetings his arrival elicited from the staff.

But when she opened her menu and saw the prices, her eyes widened in disbelief. She could practically feed herself for a month on what was charged for a meal here.

'I'll have whatever you're having,' she said weakly, snapping shut the menu and resolutely ignoring the look of exasperation he flashed her.

'Cassandra, you haven't the faintest idea what my tastes in food are,' he exclaimed impatiently. 'For heaven's sake, choose what you want—and hurry up about it, we've things to discuss.'

Bristling with indignation, she made her choice.

'I have to go to Europe for a couple of weeks,' he announced, when the waiter had taken their orders. 'Naturally I'll be in regular touch with the London office, but I think it's time you had a taste of running the Tower completely on your own.'

'That shouldn't be any problem,' she replied airily—it would be a relief not to have him breathing down her neck for a change. 'Things are running smoothly and I've made up a detailed schedule of projects taking us well into the new year.'

He frowned. 'I don't recall you showing me that.'

'I was going to this morning,' she replied, irritated by his reaction. 'Though I'm surprised you feel the need to vet something quite as basic as that, given the confidence you keep stressing you have in my abilities.'

He wasn't in the least amused by her candid observation—a fact his coldly censorious look showed plainly.

'Another thing,' he continued, pointedly ignoring her remarks. 'With Christmas less than three months away, there'll be a marked increase in social functions.'

Cassandra's look became wary as she felt her heart sink. 'But surely that sort of thing won't apply much to the Tower?'

'You seem to forget that the Tower is merely part of a much larger concern. You'll just have to accept that your social life will be on the increase pretty soon.'

'My social life?' she croaked. 'What about Lisa...or your girlfriend?'

'I don't wish to take Lisa,' he drawled mockingly. 'And as for my girlfriend, as you so quaintly put it, I seem to recall your regarding as poetic justice the fact that she's decided to sue the shirt off my back.'

'I didn't mean that one...I thought you'd have found yourself someone else by now,' she muttered, her eyes fixed on her plate.

'Well, until I do—and it might never happen—I shall be needing you.'

Ignorant though she might be about business entertaining, Cassandra strongly suspected he was exploiting her outrageously. And there wasn't a single thing she could do about it, she reminded herself bitterly—her job was far too important to her to risk arguing.

'Which brings us to the delicate question of your apparel.'

She gritted her teeth in mounting fury.

'Addicted though you obviously are to the impoverished student look, it doesn't exactly befit your position in the company. Apart from the odd business lunch that could crop up, there are also regular management meetings you'll be required to attend—and I shall expect you to be suitably dressed for both. What you wear the rest of the time is up to you.'

'Have you quite finished?' she demanded frigidly, wondering just how much more she could take.

'No—not quite,' he snapped. 'I suggest you take Lisa or one of the other girls along with you for guidance—I've already told you my opinion of your general appearance.'

'Yes, you have!' she retorted hotly. 'And at the time you at least spared me all this hypocritical rubbish about wanting me tarted up for meetings and business lunches!'

'Tarted up is the last way I wish to see you, either publicly or privately,' he drawled. 'And the fact that I'm now and then tempted by the idea of exploring a physical relationship with you has no bearing whatever on the fact that I don't like my staff—particularly those in managerial positions—swanning around looking like waifs and strays.'

Cassandra was gazing across at him in stupefied silence. It was appalling enough having to accept the fact that there was a part of her that responded to this man as though she were a mindless slave to his touch, but what she found even more devastating was the cold lack of emotion with which he referred to an act which reason and every instinct she possessed told her should be the embodiment of warmth and passion.

'Cassandra, if you still have any doubts, we could always go back to my place, where I'd be only too willing to prove to you that there's no need for me to stoop to elaborate intrigue to get you into my bed.'

Her cheeks crimson, she picked up her wine glass and drained it.

'So, until I sort out something with the company accountants, I'll make immediate arrangements to have your name added to one of my credit cards.' He leaned over and refilled her glass. 'And now we'll drink a toast to Mildred Jessel's happy retirement to Jersey... You know, I really should have suspected something was wrong when I hadn't heard from her. She's so organised, it wouldn't take her five minutes to get settled into her new place... which is something I should have realised weeks ago.'

Cassandra remained immobile for a few seconds, her mind vainly trying to adjust to his sudden switch of mood. Then she picked up her glass and once more drained it—a far wiser move, a prevailing sanity had pointed out, than emptying it over her unpredictable companion.

CHAPTER FIVE

'TIME for afternoon tea—well, coffee and Danish pastries, to be more accurate,' announced Jill Ward, shouldering open the door to Cassandra's office and entering with a laden tray.

'Pastries?' queried Cassandra, smiling uncertainly. 'Jill, it isn't your birthday, is it?' she asked, clearing a space for the tray.

Jill shook her head. 'We've dealt with everything on today's agenda, so I nipped out for these—we deserve a treat.' She handed Cassandra one of the pastries, her anxious gaze taking in the dark shadows beneath eyes hugely accentuated by stark pallor.

'Jill, this really is sweet of you,' said Cassandra, her voice catching slightly.

'To be honest, I also wanted a word with you,' admitted Jill. 'In fact, I spent a while drumming up the courage to come and face you.'

Cassandra looked at her aghast. 'You're not going to hand in your notice!'

'Of course not,' exclaimed Jill. 'You know how I love working here with you...it's just that...Cassie, I'm worried about you,' she stammered. 'I know your father died recently and I know how devastated I'd feel if anything happened to mine...but I get the feeling that recently things have been getting on top of you—it's almost as though you've been going downhill ever since Sacha's been away.'

'It's nothing to do with him!' protested Cassandra.

'I didn't mean to imply that it was,' said Jill hastily, then gave a helpless shrug. 'Look, Cassie, I'm sorry...I didn't mean to pry, but you've just as good as admitted something is wrong.'

'I suppose I have,' sighed Cassandra, almost with relief. There were so many times she had been tempted to confide in Jill, but had always held back at the last moment. 'And as for something being wrong—that's a bit of an understatement,' she added wryly. 'It's funny, but for a while I kept telling myself that things could only get worse, and sure enough they did. Then it got to a point when I honestly believed they couldn't...but they did anyway.' She picked up her cup and took a sip from it, the only thing now holding her back being where to start. 'My father died in the States—he was doing research there with some colleagues and wasn't due back in England until he took charge of the Alcaeus project. My sister, Helen, is in Boston, and as Dad's work took him around quite a bit they didn't see too much of each other. So when he was in New York for a short seminar, Helen arranged to have a weekend there with him.'

Jill watched anxiously as she listened to those curiously expressionless, almost chanted words pouring from her friend.

'He hated New York, as he did most other large cities. The crowds and the traffic unnerved him...the only things I've ever known have that effect on him.' There was a considerable pause before she continued. 'He spotted Helen where they'd arranged to meet, but he was on the other side of a busy road from her... He just walked straight out into the traffic. Several cars ploughed into one another in attempting to avoid him...but they hadn't a chance.'

'Oh, Cassie, how horrible!' gasped Jill. 'Your poor sister... seeing him die like that!'

Cassandra shook her head. 'He didn't die till almost three months later, though he never once regained consciousness. Helen had him flown from New York to a hospital near her. I went over from Athens... we were both with him when he died.'

Jill reached over and touched her hand in a wordless gesture of sympathy.

'There were several court claims resulting from the accident. It had been Dad's fault entirely and I suppose it was a miracle no one else was seriously injured.' She paused to take another sip of her coffee. 'The trouble is, freelance research was a fairly new departure for him—when he was with Harvard, they always took care of details like insurance.' She heard Jill's soft groan of disbelief and found an ingrained loyalty to her father preventing her from adding how decidedly cavalier his attitude was at the best of times to such mundane matters. 'Though, because of his strong connections with Harvard, that institution incredibly generously settled all the court claims—amounts, I should add, that Helen and I could only envisage in terms of Monopoly money.'

'And then?' probed Jill gently, as Cassandra seemed to become lost in her own troubled thoughts.

'And then... when I say he had no insurance, that included medical cover too.' A slip-up, almost unheard-of in the American medical system, had occurred when William Lestor had been admitted to the New York hospital—no one had checked on his medical cover. The error had been compounded on his transfer to Boston by that hospital's assumption that he had been cleared in New York. 'When Helen and I received the bills... again, Monopoly money was our instant reaction.'

But this time the figures were a reality that had to be faced.

'We could hardly go begging to Harvard after their previous and completely unorthodox generosity,' Cassandra continued. They had gone to the hospital administrators and laid their cards openly on the table. 'They were amazingly understanding, considering the size of the sum involved, and agreed to wait till Dad's estate had been settled.' Their father's small estate had managed to clear the New York hospital's account, but had only reduced by a fraction the Boston one. 'They bent over backwards in offering us ten years in which to pay. But, with the amount of interest involved, Helen opted for eight years... which we've since been able to reduce to five now that I'm earning so much.'

'Cassie, when you said things went on getting worse...' Jill's words trailed to an uncomfortable halt as her eyes met Cassandra's.

'Dad's research colleagues asked an old friend of his to take over his work—they actually asked him to join them for longer than my father would have been free to... which worked out very well for me as I was to caretake his London home during that time.' She gave a small shrug of hopelessness. 'He and his wife arrived back the day after Sacha went to Europe. The trouble with some types of research is that you can never guarantee where it might lead... unfortunately this particular lot has led George Malton right back to England.'

'And now you've nowhere to live,' groaned Jill.

'Actually, I managed to find somewhere a couple of days after they got back.' She had to make a conscious effort to prevent shuddering as she pictured her new home. 'The Maltons told me I was very welcome to stay, but...' She broke off abruptly.

'But they don't know about your father's debt,' stated Jill quietly.

Cassandra shook her head. Again, it was loyalty to her father that had prevented her telling them, and there was no way she could live with such a generous couple, especially one who knew her so well, without raising their suspicions as to her meagre lifestyle.

'Cassie, you haven't said what proportion of your salary you're sending back to America each month, but something tells me it was based on your not having much in the way of living expenses—am I right?'

'Yes—but I'm managing,' she muttered uncomfortably. 'The rent's very reasonable.'

'So why have you been walking around looking like a ghost for the past several days, and with those huge black smudges round your eyes?' demanded Jill severely.

'Because . . . oh, heck, it's because I've had to take an evening waitressing job. I know, I know!' she exclaimed, as Jill gave a croak of disbelief. 'I've applied for something with far fewer hours than I'm doing now— and anyway, it's only to tide me over until I get my finances sorted out.'

'Cassie, for heaven's sake, this is mad!' groaned Jill. 'Sacha's due back any day now—and those functions he mentioned start building up way before Christmas.'

'I know, but if I get this other thing it'll only involve two evenings a week.'

'And if they clash with something Sacha needs you for?'

'I—I'll tell him I'm attending evening classes or something those nights!'

Jill gave a sigh, then picked up her pastry and took a bite from it, her expression gloomy.

'Jill, I just wish I hadn't told you any of this,' exclaimed Cassandra miserably. 'All I've done is depress you.'

Jill gave a wan smile as she finished her mouthful. 'What's a bit of depression among friends?' she retorted drolly. 'And as for not telling me, all I can say is thank God I got up the courage to tackle you. They say two heads are better than one, and honestly, Cassie, you really do need someone to take you in hand... What's wrong?' she exclaimed, as Cassandra gave a sudden groan.

'You've just reminded me! There's a managerial meeting the day after tomorrow and Sacha issued orders for me to clean up my scruffy image before attending one... Would you help me choose something suitable to wear?'

'My God, that man really has got a nerve!' said Jill indignantly. 'Cassie, can you actually afford to start buying a new wardrobe?'

'He arranged for me to have a credit card,' she muttered, conscious that her colour was rising.

'Well, that's a relief,' chuckled Jill. 'Of course I'll gladly help you choose a new wardrobe if it's on... on the company.'

'No—just a dress, or perhaps a suit, will do,' said Cassandra hastily, only too conscious of Jill's slight hesitation.

'Cassie, I think it might also be an idea if we did something about your hair—and a bit of make-up.'

'Jill, you're beginning to sound just like Sacha!' she blurted out, and instantly wished she hadn't as Jill's eyes widened with unconcealed consternation.

'Cassie, all I meant was that these extra hours you've been putting in at night have taken their toll...you're looking almost haggard,' Jill pointed out gently.

'I'm sorry...you're right,' whispered Cassandra miserably.

'And I'm quite good with the scissors—perhaps if I cut a little shape into your hair you wouldn't look so...so...'

'Scruffy,' supplied Cassandra promptly.

Jill laughed as she shook her head. 'Actually I was searching for another word for haggard...drawn, perhaps,' she murmured. 'Cassie, I'm sure that whatever Sacha has said to you about your appearance was meant in a purely business context. Carmichael's has a reputation as one of the most high-powered companies around, and it's only natural he would expect his staff to reflect that.'

Cassandra picked up her pastry and took a bite from it, refraining from pointing out that Jill had, only moments before, accused him of having a nerve.

'Cassie, I'm a year younger than you—so why is it you manage to bring out the mother hen in me?' laughed Jill softly, her gentle, anxious eyes scanning Cassandra's face.

'I do?' queried Cassandra with the ghost of a smile.

'Yes, you do,' sighed Jill. 'Which is why I...' She broke off to take a deep breath, then continued, 'Cassie, I know it's not fair to judge people on rumour, but there's an awful lot of it flying around about how badly Sacha treated the girl I replaced. And the papers have been full of this love-hate relationship he's alleged to have with the woman who's suing him...Oh, heck, why on earth did I start this?' she groaned. 'Cassie, what I'm trying to say is don't for heaven's sake get in any way emotionally involved with Sacha—he's nothing but bad news where women are concerned.'

'Point taken—and with no offence, Ma,' said Cassandra, managing to produce a smile. Jill had told her nothing she hadn't already known, but the unpalatable truth was that, in the weeks Sacha had been gone, and despite the catastrophic changes taking place in her life during that time, she had missed him. Perhaps it was only in the way a long-endured pain was missed once it disappeared, she reflected edgily, but she had, none the less, missed him.

'Just hang on a minute, will you, Jill, and don't for heaven's sake distract me,' called out Cassandra as she heard the door to her office open. 'I'm just tucking the rest of those old box files out of the way up here—and I think I've just discovered what vertigo is!'

'So why the hell are you teetering on top of a step-ladder, then?' came Sacha's mildly curious tones from immediately below her.

'Sacha!' she yelped, then found herself clutching on to the top of the ladder for dear life. 'I was storing these up here to give Jill a bit more space in her office.' She gingerly eased her frantic hold on the ladder. 'How was Europe?' she added, tentatively wondering if the sudden pounding in her ears could be a symptom of her newly discovered vertigo.

'Europe was fine...Cassandra, would you mind getting off that contraption before you fall off it?'

'I've only a few more——' She broke off with a shriek of terror as he shook the ladder, then she hastily scrambled down. 'You could have broken my neck!' she accused indignantly, though her eyes became resolutely trained on the dazzling white of his shirt front, refusing to rise any further.

'Most unlikely from six feet up,' he pointed out mildly. 'Cassandra, we do have maintenance staff only too willing to carry out tasks like this.'

'I wanted it done now,' she muttered, her fixed gaze becoming suddenly distorted as he moved. 'Sacha, what on earth are you doing?' she exclaimed as she realised he had begun mounting the ladder.

'You said you wanted it done now,' he retorted, taking the files she had balanced precariously on the top rung and transferring them to the shelf.

He had rather nice legs, she noticed as her eyes now became riveted on the taut swell of flexing muscle beneath dark suiting as he stepped up and stretched.

'Any more?'

Cassandra gave a start as he spoke, horrified by this ridiculous train of thought. 'No, that's it . . . thanks.'

She had considered things bad enough before he left, she thought with a sharp stab of alarm, but at least then she hadn't sunk to drooling over his physical attributes.

'There's a managerial meeting at ten—did you remember?' he asked, descending the steps, then folding them out of the way.

'Of course I did.' The fact that she was wearing the dress she and Jill had bought only yesterday, and that not a hair of her minimally restyled head was out of place, should have made that abundantly plain, she thought crossly. Perhaps she should have given in to Jill and let her do more with her hair, she thought nervously.

'Cassandra, you look a bit peaky. Are you all right?' he asked, peering down at her with a frown.

'I'm not peaky,' she muttered defensively, suppressing a frantic urge to step back from him. 'Since you're such an expert, I'd have thought you'd realise it's just all this make-up I'm plastered with,' she added with an irritability born of unease. 'Not to mention that this outfit just isn't me, but——'

'I wouldn't go so far as to say that,' he murmured, placing a finger under her chin and forcing her head up. 'And you're not, thank God, plastered in make-up, otherwise I'd not be able to see how pale you are beneath it . . . So what gives, Cassandra?'

'Nothing gives,' she snapped, pushing his hand aside.

'No?' he mocked, suddenly reaching for her and pulling her against him. 'Don't tell me you didn't miss me, Cassandra,' he added softly, his hands sliding lightly against her back.

Though she froze to an outward stillness, inwardly she felt a treacherous warmth begin seeping languorously through her.

'Well, Cassandra?' He lowered his head, his lips brushing in tantalising lightness against hers.

Angrily she turned her face away, only to feel the soft breath of his mocking laughter against her cheek.

'I'm sure you wouldn't believe me, would you, Cassandra,' he taunted softly, his hands seductively moulding her body to his, 'were I to claim I hadn't missed you?'

Without thinking, she turned to inform him that she would be quite prepared to believe him, and found her lips trapped in the hot impatience of his waiting mouth.

The groan that was torn from her as her arms rose to cling was one of helpless acquiescence. But it was the sharp exclamation of surprise, followed by hastily muttered words of apology, coming from behind them that tore them apart, spinning them both round.

Cassandra felt herself freeze in a sickened numbness of disbelief as she glimpsed Jill's figure before the door fully closed.

'I hope you're satisfied!' she hurled at him, humiliation shattering through her numbness.

'I can't help it if your assistant chooses to barge in unannounced,' he drawled, removing a handkerchief from his pocket and wiping her lipstick from his mouth with it. 'Anyway, it's hardly the end of the world, is it?' he added unconcernedly, glancing down at the stained handkerchief in his hand.

'Perhaps not for you,' cried out Cassandra wildly. 'But you make me feel like...like a *whore*! All right, so it gives you some sort of perverted kick to prove how easily you can manipulate women. And all right, so I'm the same as all the rest of them...but why did you have to humiliate me by proving that point in front of Jill?'

'Cassandra, stop being so hysterical! How the hell was I to know she'd walk in?' he demanded, his eyes narrowing in alarmed disbelief as they scrutinised her distraught features. 'God, this is ridiculous!' he exclaimed impatiently, grasping her by the arm and dragging her over to the chair by her desk. 'Cassandra, sit down.' He pushed her unceremoniously down on to the chair when she showed no signs of complying, then strode towards the door. 'Jill!' he bellowed.

Cassandra closed her eyes and turned her face away, a major part of her unable to believe this was really happening to her.

'Jill, is there any chance of some coffee before Cassandra and I go off to this meeting?' she heard him say as the door opened. 'I'm afraid I've behaved badly and upset her.'

Cassandra's eyes flew open in startled disbelief, just in time to see Sacha disappearing into the outer office.

'What you just witnessed was me greeting Cassandra with what started off as a peck on the cheek,' his voice carried to her, 'but somehow it didn't quite end up that way... Perhaps I got carried away by her new, super-efficient image,' he continued in tentative tones that lacked any trace of the conviction for which he had so earnestly striven.

Unable to catch Jill's softly spoken reply, Cassandra leaned back wearily on the chair. Just about everything about him disturbed and alarmed her, she thought dejectedly. And most disturbing and alarming of all was that elusive side of him that could fill him with remorse over his neglect of Mrs Jessel and which now had driven him into this unlikely charade to allay the perfectly understandable suspicions undoubtedly awakened in Jill.

She glanced up as the door swung fully open, an almost fatalistic feeling of calm pervading her as Sacha, with Jill at his heels, entered bearing a tray.

'I asked Jill to join us,' he announced, his eyes almost pleading as they met hers. 'Not because you need the services of a chaperon, but because... well, I just thought it would be nice if she joined us.' Having made that to-tally uncharacteristic and garbled statement, he promptly slipped right back into character by rolling his eyes in pained disbelief at the sound of his own words.

One glimpse of Jill's face, and the amusement threat-ening to run amok over it, told Cassandra precisely how her assistant had reacted to that hammed charade.

And one look at the discomfort in Sacha's eyes gave her the answer to what so disturbed and alarmed her.

She might have been safe had she never seen it—that elusive, so fatally appealing side of him. But she had seen it, and was in grave danger of losing her heart to it.

CHAPTER SIX

CASSANDRA undressed, chanting silent words of encouragement to herself as she donned what was euphemistically referred to as her uniform.

'You know, I swear this wretched outfit shrinks by the minute,' she muttered as she buttoned the bibbed top of a minuscule frilly apron.

She turned to survey herself in the full-length mirror, still half convinced, as she had been on both other occasions, that it was someone other than herself she was seeing. Her legs, clad in black fishnet tights, seemed grotesquely long. Well, they would, she thought disdainfully, exaggerated as they were by six-inch black stiletto shoes and the fact that the excuse for a skirt she had to wear was barely the length of those ridiculous heels on which she could only teeter.

'Cheer up, Cass. You have to admit that it isn't quite as bad as we first dreaded—not that anything could have been that bad,' chuckled the tall brunette in an identical outfit.

'Oh no?' muttered Cassandra. 'The only good thing about out there is that the lighting is so appalling people can hardly see us—a blessing easily cancelled out by the likelihood of my breaking a leg staggering around in it.'

Anne Collyer gave a sympathetic grin. A student finding it impossible to make ends meet on her grant, Anne had suggested they look around for something less exhaustingly time-consuming than the waitressing that had brought them together. And it had been Anne who had found them their present work, but who still suffered pangs of doubt as to the wisdom of having talked Cassandra into taking it.

'Anne, I honestly don't think I'm ever going to get used to lurching around out there on these stilts and holding my breath at the same time.'

There was affection in Anne's puzzled smile as she watched Cassandra's painstaking adjustment of the apron top.

'I'm sure you must have a perfectly valid reason for the breath-holding,' she remarked. 'It's just that I can't for the life of me think what it could be.'

'It's quite simple.' Cassandra grinned. 'If I don't hold my breath I might just as well be topless—it's the only way I can keep this ridiculous bib in place.' She turned to her companion with a hopeful look. 'Anne, you wouldn't by any chance happen to have some sticky-tape on you?' She blinked in bemusement as Anne became convulsed with laughter.

'Sorry—I'm afraid you'll just have to keep on holding your breath, Cass.'

'Oh, well, here goes,' sighed Cassandra. 'It's about time we were entering the lions' den,' she added reluctantly, then took an exaggerated breath that immediately reduced Anne to paroxysms of laughter once more.

At least they managed to extract a bit of humour from the whole ghastly thing, thought Cassandra, desperately seeking a scrap of comfort to boost her on her way to one of the three tables she served. But no amount of humour could ever lessen the cringing sense of humiliation that writhed non-stop inside her as she began taking orders.

Remembering Anne's sanity-preserving tips, she kept her eyes glued to the pad on which she wrote, never once allowing them to leave it.

'Try to avoid any eye contact with them and pretend not to hear if they start wisecracking,' Anne had advised. 'And, above all, remember they're paying a small fortune to see the cabaret and they're out on their ears, with no refund, if they get fresh with the waitresses.'

It had been the management's boast that no customer had ever laid a finger on one of the girls, together with the exceptionally high wages offered, that had helped Cassandra override the shrieking protests emanating from the very core of her being at the idea of even considering such a job. But beggars couldn't afford to be choosers, she reminded herself unnecessarily as she handed in the orders. And without this supplementary income begging could well be on the cards.

Gingerly she made her way towards her next table, grateful for the dimness of the lighting, but again wondering how long it would be before either it or the wretched shoes caused her to go sprawling.

'Would you like to place your orders?' she recited tonelessly.

'Good God almighty—I don't believe this!'

It was the mind-numbing familiarity of that voice that startled her into breaking her rule—she looked. And she found herself looking down into the outraged eyes of Sacha.

'Oh, hell!' she croaked, then took the only option available to her. She dropped both pad and pencil and fled.

'Oh no you don't!' he snarled, his hand an arresting vice on her arm before she had taken more than a couple of steps.

'Let go of the girl, sir.'

Cassandra began praying the floor would open up and swallow her as she heard that polite request from the burly bouncer, who then gently but firmly removed Sacha's hand from her arm.

'I'm OK,' she assured her would-be protector, forcing a smile to the numbed rigidity of her lips.

Still attempting to smile placatingly at the bouncer, in a purely reflex reaction she managed to catch the dinner-jacket the scowling Sacha had shrugged from his shoulders and flung at her.

'Cover yourself!' he spat at her, his voice tight with fury.

'I'm afraid I shall have to ask you to leave the premises,' stated the bouncer.

Cassandra hurled herself at Sacha's arm, tugging frantically at it as, his face ashen with rage, he swung round to confront the other man.

'Sacha, come on—let's go,' she pleaded, still tugging on his arm while at the same time desperately trying to retain her balance on the ludicrous heels. 'Well, I suppose I might as well say goodbye to that job,' she muttered with the inanity of shock, once she had succeeded in dragging him into the foyer.

'Job?' he exploded, spinning her round to face him and sending his jacket flying from her shoulders. 'I harboured the delusion that you worked for me,' he snarled, retrieving the jacket and throwing it around her once more, 'not as a tart in a strip joint!'

His arm was a punishing weight on her shoulders, holding his jacket in place and forcing her to keep pace with his long, angry strides as he marched her outside.

'You know perfectly well it isn't a strip joint,' she protested, trying desperately to whip up anger or any other feeling that could hold at bay the terrible humiliation threatening to engulf her. 'You've no right to——'

'Shut up and get in!' he rasped, opening the passenger door and virtually shoving her into his car.

'You've absolutely no right to treat me like this!' she choked, panic welling in her as she scrambled to get the door open.

'You're wasting your time,' he informed her harshly, sliding into the driver's seat and slamming his door. 'It's a central locking system and so the lock's childproof— a fact I find somewhat ironic right at this very moment.'

She flashed him a look of total incomprehension, one that quickly turned to alarm as the powerful car roared to life.

'Don't tell me the irony is wasted on a bright girl like you, Cassandra,' he drawled venomously. 'Not when you've gone to such extraordinary lengths to fabricate this picture for me of yourself as a helpless, rather endearing child. And I have to admit you did it with such skill that you almost had me fooled!'

The look of total incomprehension returned to her face, while a blank sense of desolation crept over and enshrouded her.

'Sacha, wherever you're going,' she said tonelessly, 'I should point out that my clothes are still back there.'

She glanced over at the grim set of his profile, wondering if he had heard what she said. Of course he had heard, she told herself numbly, while that charged silence lengthened between them, slowly bringing with it stark realisation of what had taken place and the utter devastation its repercussions were about to wreak on her life.

'Sacha...' she began in a sudden surge of panic, then slumped back against the seat in hopeless resignation.

His actually uttering the words to fire her would be an unnecessary formality. She must have been out of her mind even to think she could get away with it, she berated herself as the silence closed ever more suffocatingly around her... It had only been a matter of time before someone connected with Carmichael's had spotted her there.

'For God's sake say something!' she blurted out, unable to take the silence any longer.

His reaction was instant and terrifying. He slammed on the brakes, jarring the car to so sharp a standstill she was hurled painfully against the seatbelt.

'If you had an iota of sense you'd understand with what difficulty I'm holding my tongue!' he rasped. 'For both our sakes I intend being in complete control of myself before risking any exchange with you.'

'You could at least tell me where we're going,' she protested, as he swung the car back into the traffic.

'To your place,' he snapped, fury glittering unabated in the depths of his eyes.

Her heart, already in the vicinity of her stomach, plunged further. 'You're going in the wrong direction.' With no choice but to do so, she gave him her new address.

And when they eventually arrived she saved herself the bother of voicing any protest as he followed her into the dingy hall and up the endless, filth-stained flights of stairs.

To mask the all-pervading stench of stale cabbage that seemed to ooze from the very walls, she had taken to burning joss-sticks in her room, and she was grateful to be greeted by that pungent Eastern smell as she opened the door and switched on the light. And because words would be futile she offered none, but she was unable to stop herself watching and waiting for his reaction as he followed her in and surveyed the tiny room.

She saw his eyes skim from the iron-framed single bed with its frayed cover to the heavy, rickety wardrobe that stood, as it had since her arrival, with its doors wide open in an attempt to rid it of its damp mustiness. She followed his eyes as they then moved to the drab chest of drawers on which rested one of her still-unpacked cases, then on towards the chair on which lay the second. And as she watched him, tall and remote, yet strangely exotic in contrast to the dismal drabness surrounding him, she witnessed the colour drain slowly from his face.

No word was spoken by either of them as he stepped forward and closed first one, then the other of her cases and placed them on the floor at his feet.

'If you have anything else here, get it,' he ordered, his tone ominously quiet. 'You're leaving this place.' Taking a case in each hand, he walked to the door.

'Sacha, all this drama is pointless,' she said wearily. 'I happen to live here. Just put my cases back where you found them and go!' Her last words were called frantically from the landing as he began descending the stairs.

'Sacha!' she beseeched, teetering precariously on the six-inch heels as she clattered down the stairs after him.

Ignoring her increasingly frantic calls, he marched straight out of the front door, continuing even when she gave a cry of fright as she lost her footing and tumbled down the rest of the stairs.

'Well, this is a nice carry-on to be having in the middle of the night!'

Cassandra looked up, tears of pain and frustration glinting in her eyes as she saw the dressing-gowned figure of her landlady. She made an attempt to rise, then felt her head begin to swim as a sickening pain stabbed through the ankle twisted beneath her.

'There are certain types we don't like here,' the landlady informed her, open disdain in the eyes taking in Cassandra's near-nakedness. 'I thought I'd made that perfectly clear when you came here. You'll have to——'

'Miss Lestor won't have to anything,' interrupted Sacha's ice-cold voice. 'She's leaving anyway.'

Almost shouldering the woman aside, he retrieved his jacket from the stairs and for the third time that evening it was placed around Cassandra's shoulders.

'She can't just leave,' objected the woman. 'She'll have to give a month's rent as notice.'

'But I've already paid three months in advance—and a deposit,' gasped Cassandra, her eyes refusing to meet those of Sacha squatting beside her as she hugged the jacket tightly round her.

'You'll have to——' The woman's threat came to an abrupt halt as Sacha rose menacingly to his feet. 'I'll call the police,' she blustered.

'You do that,' advised Sacha coldly, reaching down and pulling Cassandra upright. 'For God's sake take those bloody shoes off!' he exclaimed as she fell against him.

'Sacha...I've done something to my ankle,' she groaned, turning a deathly white. 'I can't put any weight on it.'

With a muttered oath, he lifted her up into his arms and strode out, leaving the landlady muttering threats at his retreating back.

When he had seated Cassandra in the car he knelt down and examined her ankle. 'This shoe will have to come off—the strap's cutting into your flesh.'

With a gentleness totally at variance with the clenched set of his jaw, he undid both shoes and eased her feet free. He then closed the passenger door and, having hurled both shoes at the door through which he had just carried her, he got into the car.

'That ankle might need some attention,' he observed prosaically.

It was the utter incongruity of his tone that proved the last straw, destroying the frail dam within her holding at bay the fear, the full awareness of the merciless pain throbbing in her leg and, most of all, realisation of the hopeless mess her entire life was now in.

'My ankle?' she whispered. 'My ankle...' Her words were lost in a choked sob and the sudden rush of tears—but she no longer cared. Why should she? She had tried to cope with something that had been impossible from the start, so why bother about a few tears now that it was all over?

'A bit hackneyed, but a nice try anyway, Cassandra,' he snarled, taking her by the shoulders and shaking her with a cold fury that brought an instant end to her tears. 'That's better,' he observed grimly, his face a blur to her tear-washed eyes.

Then his mouth was on hers, harsh and insistent as it bruised the soft vulnerability of the lips that parted to its loveless search.

Like one responding to a potent drug that erased reality, she gave herself up to the need surging to instant life within her, reaching up to let her fingers tangle in the glossy darkness of his hair. And she became lost completely when his hands moved to cup her breasts, the teasing torment of his caressing fingers sending sharp waves of desire coursing through her. When gentleness gave way to demanding urgency in the maddening caress of those hands, the shivering response with which her body replied brought an incoherent groan from the lips goading hers to wanton desperation.

When those hands ceased their tormenting caress, reaching up to imprison and remove the hands still clinging round his neck, and when he then drew his body from hers, the cold harshness of reality reached out to claim her once more.

'It's strange, isn't it?' he stated in a voice distorted by hoarseness. 'The only time I can be really sure that your acting skills play no part is when you're in my arms.'

Her acting skills, she mused with a peculiarly detached weariness. Earlier he had spoken in equally scathing tones of the picture he believed her to have fabricated of herself. She tried to shake her head in an attempt to clear it, but it refused to respond. In the past couple of weeks, in fact, ever since the scene in her office the day he had returned from Europe, it had been the conspicuous lack of wariness, of suspicion almost, in his eyes that had brought home to her its previous existence. Some people always seemed to know instinctively when they were being lied to—perhaps he was one of them. And she had probably told him more lies since she had worked for him than she had told in total in her life before. But never colossal, earth-shattering lies... Had she been free to tell him her secret from the outset, the need for most of those lies would never have existed.

'Whatever plot you're hatching in that scheming little head of yours, forget it, Cassandra,' he informed her brutally. 'Because, from now on, I'm the one calling all the tunes.'

He gunned the car back to life, but she was too lost in the morass of her thoughts even to notice the hair-raising speed at which they took off.

Tonight she had lost not only a job she loathed, but doubtless the one she loved, and, what was more, she no longer had a roof over her head. She pressed a clenched hand against her mouth and without warning was reliving the fire of his mouth against her own and the caress of his hands burning once more against her skin. There was definitely something drastically wrong with her sense of priority, she accused herself agitatedly. Her life was in virtual shreds and yet here she was, wallowing in the memory of his touch and hurt beyond reason that he regarded her as a calculating schemer. It wasn't as though he had ever made any secret of the contempt with which he viewed women, she reminded herself angrily, so why should she expect to be regarded differently? She jammed her knuckles fiercely against her mouth, welcoming the pain as an accusing voice inside her reminded her of how easy it would have been to love the gentler, less aggressive Sacha of the past couple of weeks. But that wasn't the true Sacha, she reminded herself bitterly, and kept on reminding herself until, by the time they had drawn up before a white-walled mews cottage, she had come partially to her senses.

There was no way she could ever love him. She desired him, undoubtedly, but there were times, such as this very moment, when she actively loathed him.

'Where exactly are we?' she demanded, the loathing naked in her eyes as she faced him.

'By "exactly", are you asking me to recite the address, or would the information that it's my home suffice?'

'Well, thanks for the lift,' she retorted with weary flippancy. 'If you'd kindly get me my cases, I'll be off.'

'Oh, really? Where to?' he enquired as he removed the keys from the ignition.

'It's none of your business,' she replied haughtily, ruthlessly suppressing a vivid mental picture of herself staggering through the streets of London, a case in each hand, and in her present attire. Of course, she could always change in a park or somewhere, she told herself, a thought from which she derived no comfort whatever.

'Unfortunately it's very much my business, not that it's something I have any intention of sitting out here discussing.' He got out of the car and went round to the passenger side. 'No arguing—out!'

'Go to hell!'

His face suffused with fury, he hoisted her from the car and slammed the door shut.

Befuddled by outrage, she placed her weight on both feet, a soft moan escaping her as an excruciating pain in her left ankle sent her toppling backwards against the car.

She made no sound as he grasped her by the upper thighs, then heaved her over his shoulder.

She heard the slam of the front door behind them and felt the sudden sensation of warmth, but she saw nothing of the house they had entered because her eyes were now tightly shut. And they remained shut even as she felt herself deposited, none too gently, on a cushioned surface.

'Cassandra, the first thing you're going to do before we discuss anything is have a bath. I'll get you a robe.'

She heard the sound of his departing footsteps, her mind devoid of thought, her eyes still tightly shut.

'Here—put this on and I'll help you upstairs to the bathroom.'

She felt something soft land on her, but gave no re-action. It was better—safer—like this, cocooned in darkness and silence.

'Snap out of it, Cassandra,' he rasped, anger and impatience in his tone. 'Your foot's a mess, and we're probably going to have to cut those damned tights off you.'

We? She struggled up, her eyes flying open.

'I'm perfectly capable of getting out of them myself,' she informed him frigidly, and began struggling into the large white towelling robe lying across her.

The sudden movement brought an involuntary gasp of pain from her, and when she gazed down at her throbbing ankle her eyes widened in horror. The heavy fishnet tights were clinging like a vice to her swollen flesh, cutting deeply into it.

'I'd better get a doctor in to have a look at it in the morning,' Sacha stated brusquely. 'Meanwhile, a soak in a hot bath won't do it any harm.' He helped her to her feet. 'I'll carry you—you'll never manage the stairs.'

She made no protest as he swung her effortlessly into his arms. But it was the impersonal hold of those arms that began chipping at the brittle veneer so precariously protecting her. So short a while ago, those same arms had held her in passion. A passion he had ruthlessly doused almost as quickly as it had flared, she reminded herself with bitter humiliation as he carried her into a bathroom off a large, airy bedroom and placed her on a stool.

She watched his businesslike economy of movement as he rolled up the sleeves of his ornate dress-shirt and began running the bath—the incongruity of it all filling her with a strange sense of detachment. And she watched in that same detached silence as he rummaged in a mir-rored cabinet, then handed her a pair of scissors.

'Do you want me to do it?'

'No, I can...thank you,' she muttered awkwardly as she took the scissors.

'Are you going to be OK getting into the bath?'

She nodded, her feeling of detachment total, and to her relief he left the room.

She got into the bath with considerable difficulty, then lay back and let the hot water soothe her aching body.

For several minutes she lay there, her mind refusing to abandon its role of uninvolved spectator, until a sudden mental picture of her sister dragged her back to her senses. Helen, with her uncomplaining stoicism, had managed to honour her part of the deal, and even though Helen herself had pointed out that she had already had a good job when all this had blown up in their faces, nothing could alter the fact that it was she, Cassandra, who had let them down so catastrophically. And soon she would have to face Sacha's inevitable demands for an explanation.

As hopelessness washed over her, she toyed with the idea of telling him the truth, discarding it the instant she envisaged his look of cynical disbelief and heard his scathing words of derision ringing in her head. Confiding in Jill had been a safety-valve she had desperately needed, but to tell Sacha the truth and to hear him dismiss it as a lie was something she couldn't bring herself to face... He regarded her as a calculating schemer, so how else could he possibly react?

She stepped out of the bath, wincing from the pain shooting through her leg as she put a minimal amount of weight on it. And even had there been the remotest chance that he might have believed her, there was nothing to be gained from telling him the truth when it went without saying that she had already lost her job with his company.

She swaddled herself in the robe and, using the wall to support herself, opened the door and hopped through to the bedroom.

Sacha was standing by the bed, the covers of which were now drawn back.

'You might as well get into bed,' he pointed out coldly, his eyes flickering over her with complete indifference. 'You've nowhere else to go.'

She opened her mouth to object, then closed it. Why bother? As he had so succinctly pointed out, she had nowhere else to go.

Humiliation a sickening knot in the pit of her stomach, she eased herself on to the bed, her eyes registering nothing as they happened to catch sight of the puffy distortion of her foot.

'Do you want to try bandaging it for support?' he demanded, his gaze following hers.

She shook her head. 'If you wouldn't mind, I'd like to get all this over and done with,' she stated, lunging straight to the point before her nerves deserted her. 'I realise it was completely irresponsible of me to take that sort of evening work while being employed by a company such as Carmichael's. But, in case you're worried, I'll make sure that Jill has all the information she needs to cope without me.'

'Something tells me we've been here before,' he snapped impatiently. 'Am I to understand, from what you've just said, that you're resigning?'

Cassandra blinked several times in confusion, then her face tightened with anger. 'OK, if you want to make a meal of firing me, go ahead—indulge yourself!'

'The question of firing you hasn't even entered my head.'

Her eyes were dark with suspicion as she gazed up at him. 'Are you actually saying...I can still keep my job?' she croaked.

'Your job at the Tower,' he snapped, drawing a fragilely elegant, velvet-cushioned chair towards the bed and sitting down. There was a total lack of expression in his face, as he leaned back and watched her, that threw her completely. 'You work for me, and for no one else—is that clear?'

Cassandra attempted to nod and found her neck muscles refusing to co-operate.

'And whatever kicks you derive from working in the sort of dive I found you in tonight——'

'Kicks?' she gasped in horror. 'You can't possibly believe any woman in her right mind would work in a place like that for kicks!'

'So you were doing it for the money,' he murmured with chilling softness.

'Of course I was doing it for the money!' she exploded. 'What sort of person do you take me for?'

A cold smile crept to his lips as his eyes met hers in open mockery.

'Do you really want me to answer that, Cassandra?' he taunted. 'Anyway, this money you owe—I can only assume you are in some sort of debt—how much is it?'

'Why do you ask?' she blurted out without thinking.

'Obviously because I intend settling whatever it is—but I'm sure you were banking on my doing so sooner or later... Isn't that what any sensible woman would expect of a man of means who desires her?'

Moments before those final words of his had knocked the breath from her with the savagery of their impact, several thoughts had begun chasing chaotically through her mind. The first, almost comical in its crazy temptation, had been to quote the full figure of the debt her father had left and then to revel in Sacha's reaction. Except that there would probably have been little reaction for her to revel in, it had rapidly occurred to her; the wealthy could afford to be blasé about sums that she and Helen found astronomical. But, as the full force of his deliberate insult hit her, it was the realisation that, with the knowledge that her job was secure, she had actually considered telling him the truth that filled her with a sickening horror.

'Come, now, Cassandra, don't be coy,' he drawled.

'You're mistaken...I haven't any debts,' she whispered hoarsely.

'Yet you deny working there just for the kicks.'

'You're disgusting! What——'

'So why were you working there?'

'I...because...it's my sister's birthday in——' it was Helen's birthday in April, she thought frantically '—soon, and I wanted to get her a really nice birthday present.' It was Christmas soon, raged her dulled reason, why couldn't she have said Christmas instead of dragging fictitious birthdays into it? 'A combined birthday and Christmas present,' she added, feeling like pulling the bedclothes over her head and giving up the ghost as the utter falseness of her own tones danced accusingly in her ears.

'Cassandra, I'd like you to tell me something,' he informed her quietly, 'and I'd rather you didn't lie, especially as it's something I can verify should I feel the need. How much were they paying you for displaying your considerable physical assets at that place?'

Her cheeks hot with shame, she tossed the figure at him.

'That little?' he muttered, so quietly she almost missed the words.

She gave a mental shrug—to her it had seemed a small fortune, but then most things were relative.

'Right—here's my offer.'

She stiffened, instinctively bracing herself.

'I'll round that figure up.' The sum he mentioned was one far in excess of what she had been earning at the nightclub. 'And I'm prepared to pay you that amount for as long as you remain here.'

'For as long as I remain here?' she croaked, her mouth like sandpaper.

'You move in here as—how shall I put it?' he mused, a cold parody of a smile chilling his features. 'As my social hostess. I've never particularly enjoyed the endless round of entertaining in which I'm required to be involved, especially towards this time of the year. And quite frankly there are times when I get sick and tired of the sight of restaurants. I much prefer to do my entertaining here at home.' His eyes narrowed as they flickered across her startled face. 'And I'm sure you won't have the same problems poor Deborah experienced with Mrs Edgar— my housekeeper.' He paused, his brows rising in faint query as Cassandra's head began shaking from side to side in total incomprehension. 'I'd better explain—Mrs Edgar is the exception that proves every rule there is about women. And the ravishing Deborah wasn't intelligent enough to realise that the woman who runs my house and cooks for me will always win hands down over any other... something I'm sure you won't have any problem understanding.'

Cassandra made a hopeless gesture of complete bewilderment, half convinced this could be nothing more than a bad dream.

'It's perfectly simple,' he snapped. 'You move in here, into what many might consider the lap of luxury, and in return you perform the duties of a hostess when re-

quired...for which I pay you the sum agreed. Just think
of all the magnificent presents you'll be able to send
your sister, and not only for her birthday and
Christmas——'

'Sacha, I——'

'Before you say anything,' he cut in imperiously, 'I
should point out that this arrangement finishes when I
decide it does, and not once you've finished indulging
your remarkable generosity towards your sister—
understood?'

There was one thing she had no option but to understand, she realised numbly—that she had no alternative
but to accept this loaded offer of his.

'Yes, but I don't want your money——'

'Oh, come, now, Cassandra——'

'I'll stay here and I'll act as your hostess when you
entertain...but nothing more!'

He rose, his mocking eyes sweeping over her huddled
form. 'Nothing more?' he laughed in soft disbelief. 'You
may not realise it, but it just isn't in my nature to use
force...which is why I find it such a comfort knowing
that whatever I want will be there for the taking.'

In that moment she experienced none of the problems
she had hitherto had in defining her feelings towards
him—they were of loathing, pure and simple...and, for
that brief moment, it was a knowledge from which she
gained a minute grain of comfort.

CHAPTER SEVEN

'KEEP the weight off it for two or three days and it should be fine.' The doctor slid the tooled leather pouffe under Cassandra's neatly bandaged foot. 'It's quite a nasty sprain, but fortunately there's nothing broken. I'd better go and ring Mr Carmichael with the good news now—he seemed rather worried when he contacted me this morning.'

Well, bully for Sacha! thought Cassandra bitterly as she lay back against the cushions of the pale velvet sofa, the one on which that same caring Sacha had deposited her last night, she told herself irritably as her eyes swept round the room.

Creams and subtle greens combined with the delicate elegance of walnut to give an air of light and serenity to a room that was large and exquisitely furnished.

She adjusted her foot slightly, feeling the soft material of the navy caftan she was wearing, the first thing that had come to hand when she had dressed that morning, and she sighed.

There had been no sign of Sacha when she had hobbled down the stairs earlier. She glanced at her watch. He would have been at the office for several hours now...and her own day threatened to take forever, just lying around here doing nothing, she fretted. It had begun with the arrival of a plump, grey-haired woman bearing a breakfast tray and introducing herself as Mrs Edgar. And the housekeeper had shown no surprise at her presence, Cassandra remembered, the wry thought only then occurring to her that any surprise the woman might have felt would have been at finding her in the spare room instead of Sacha's bed.

'I thought you might feel like a nice cup of coffee after your ordeal.'

Cassandra looked up, to find Mrs Edgar now approaching her.

'That smells wonderful,' she murmured as the tempting aroma of freshly brewed coffee wafted to her.

'The doctor's on the phone to Mr Sacha—how does the leg feel now?' the housekeeper asked sympathetically.

'Much better now that it's been strapped up,' replied Cassandra shyly, embarrassed to remember her certainty of the previous night that this motherly woman would be something of an ogress.

'Mr Sacha won't be home for lunch, but I've some nice lamb cutlets I could grill for you.'

Cassandra opened her mouth to speak, and to her utter consternation felt the breath choke in her throat and the scalding prickle of tears in her eyes.

'You drink your coffee,' advised Mrs Edgar, her kindly eyes missing nothing. 'And we'll talk about lunch later... You're bound not to feel yourself for a while after the nasty tumble you've taken.'

It was not much later, when she decided she could take no more of being alone with her disturbing, comfortless thoughts, that Cassandra hobbled her way out of that elegant, alien sitting-room and eventually found her way into the kitchen.

'Isn't there something I could do to help?' she pleaded. 'I'm just not used to sitting around twiddling my thumbs like this.'

The housekeeper gave an understanding chuckle. 'Well, just as long as Mr Sacha doesn't catch you on your feet,' she twinkled. 'I was going to do some baking—he has quite a sweet tooth at times.'

Though it was a kitchen that appeared to contain every conceivable modern appliance to be had, there was also a warmth and a homeliness about it that gradually imparted itself to Cassandra.

Surrounded by the comforting smells of good home baking and with Mrs Edgar's encouraging words to guide her, she found herself sifting ingredients and filling baking trays and, most surprising of all, chatting freely.

'Are you sure I haven't rolled these too thickly?' she asked hours later, her eyes sparkling and a warm glow bringing life to her cheeks.

'They're just right. I think we'll make a cook out of you yet,' Mrs Edgar reassured her.

'I don't know about that,' sighed Cassandra, conscious of how much she was enjoying herself. 'I'm afraid I never went in for it much—Helen's such a good cook.'

It was her casual mention of her sister that brought it to her just how much about herself she had told the kindly no-nonsense housekeeper in so relatively short a time. And it had been Mrs Edgar's occasionally pursed lips and indignant tutting noises that had once or twice made very plain her thoughts about William Lestor's eccentric upbringing of his two daughters.

'Well, with a few lessons from me I dare say you'll be able to surprise that sister of yours the next time you see her,' Mrs Edgar said, popping the last of the biscuits into the oven. 'Once those are done I'll put in that hotpot for your and Mr S's supper,' she added as she began clearing up.

'Do you prepare something for him every night?' asked Cassandra.

'Dear me, no—he's hardly ever in,' laughed the woman. 'And there's a man who could teach you a thing or two when it comes to cooking—not that he has much time for it, with him being so busy.'

'So it's just as well he has someone as brilliant as you are at it to look after him,' said Cassandra, smiling, surprised to learn of Sacha's unexpected talent. 'But there's one thing I can do, and that's make a good cup of tea,' she added. 'And I intend making us both one right now— so no arguing,' she insisted when the housekeeper began shaking her head dubiously. 'I've had my foot propped up on this stool for so long now, it's likely to take root!'

When Mrs Edgar had cleaned up to her meticulous standards, she sat down, on Cassandra's insistence, at the large, scrubbed kitchen table, and was served her tea.

'Just call me Hopalong,' Cassandra giggled as she made her ungainly way back to the table.

'The idea was that you rest,' stated a disapproving voice from the doorway.

Cassandra turned to see Sacha, still in a heavy overcoat, enter the kitchen.

'Good evening, Mrs E, I see you've had your hands full,' he observed drily.

'Miss Cassandra's been giving me a hand,' laughed the housekeeper, rising and getting a third cup. 'It was lonely for her cooped up all by herself in the sitting-room—tea?'

'Thanks.' Sacha shed his coat and draped it over one of the chairs. 'How's the foot?' he enquired of Cassandra as he took a seat.

'Much better, thank you,' she replied, only now appreciating the uncomplicated tranquillity of the past few hours as her edginess and anxiety returned with a vengeance.

'There's a hotpot in the oven for later,' announced Mrs Edgar, handing him a cup. 'But I'm sure a couple of these won't spoil your appetite,' she added with a chuckle, producing a plate laden with a selection of her afternoon's efforts.

'Mrs E, if you weren't already spoken for, I'd have no option but to marry you myself.' Sacha grinned, helping himself with boyish relish.

It was only after the housekeeper had left that he fixed eyes on Cassandra that chilled the last vestiges of warmth from her, and remarked, 'A most intelligent move, that, Cassandra, worming your way into Mrs E's affections— but it won't cut any ice with me.'

Sacha's disconcerting and altogether humiliating tendency to give only the most minimal acknowledgement to Cassandra's presence in his home ended in explosive suddenness the day she was to return to work.

The first hint of what lay in store was the look of grim dissatisfaction she received at breakfast, having entered the dining-room clad in a short faded denim skirt and navy sweatshirt. But it wasn't until they were about to leave and she had begun donning her lightweight raincoat that he erupted.

'The outfit's horrific enough, but I have to draw the line at that bloody thing!' he fumed. 'Haven't you a decent coat? It's winter, for God's sake!'

'No, I haven't a decent coat,' she chanted through clenched teeth.

'Why didn't you get yourself one? Damn it, I arranged for you to have a credit card for the express purpose of your getting clothes with it!' he exclaimed. 'Exactly what *have* you bought on it?'

'The dress I wore to the managerial meeting,' she retorted, trying desperately to keep her voice down for fear of Mrs Edgar hearing.

With a muttered exclamation of disbelief, he grabbed her by the arm and hustled her out of the house. 'Clear what you can of your work by eleven,' he ordered, handing her into the car. 'And be in my office by then. If you can't be bothered to do your shopping for yourself, it seems I'll have to do it for you.'

'I beg your pardon?' she croaked, praying she had misheard.

'I'll choose your damned clothes myself. And prepare yourself for a marathon, because we're getting them all today, no matter how long it takes.'

'Please yourself,' she muttered resignedly, then added with a flash of vindictiveness, 'Though I'd have thought a high-powered tycoon such as you would have had better things to do with his precious time.'

'And how right you'd be,' he snarled. 'Which is why I intend wasting no more than a day of it on you.'

'What a shame Deborah didn't leave behind the wardrobe you doubtless selected for her,' she murmured sweetly. 'Think of all the trouble it would have saved you.'

'Planning on stepping into Deborah's shoes, are you, Cassandra?' he enquired silkily. 'Are you that confident they'd fit?'

Cassandra clamped her mouth tightly shut—she had walked straight into that one, she informed herself angrily—and spent the rest of the journey to the office wrestling with the vivid pictures her mind kept presenting her of svelte and dauntingly beautiful women whose magnificent clothes would do little or nothing for her.

'Don't forget—eleven in my office,' he reminded her brusquely as they parted in the foyer.

It was Jill's ecstatic welcome only moments later that highlighted a recent and most disturbingly uncharacteristic tendency in her, that of her eyes filling with the threat of tears for no discernible reason.

She began busily rummaging around in her desk in an attempt to pull herself together.

'I'm afraid we haven't time for explanations right now,' she mumbled, when Jill demanded to know what had happened. 'I have all the backlog of the past few days to clear before eleven—I have to report to Sacha then.'

'Backlog? What backlog?' teased Jill. 'Didn't I say we had this place running like clockwork? Actually, I was easily able to deal with what little there was—and there doesn't seem to be anything earth-shattering in this morning's post either.'

They sorted through what the post had brought them in less than an hour.

'You prop up that foot and I'll go and get us a coffee,' said Jill. 'You're still limping a bit, you know,' she added as she went into her own office to get the coffee. 'I hope you saw a doctor.'

'Don't worry, Sacha had one standing on the doorstep as dawn broke the next morning,' she muttered drily, then gave a silent groan as she realised what she had said. 'Jill?' she called tentatively. There was no chance she hadn't heard, not with the door wide open as it was, she thought frustratedly.

'I'll be with you in a tick, Cassie.'

But she was conscious of Jill's eyes studiously avoiding hers when she returned with two steaming mugs.

'Yes, Jill, I am staying at Sacha's place—and no, it most definitely isn't the way it probably looks.'

She then told Jill all that had happened, omitting only anything pertaining to her own fatalistic fear, and Sacha's mortifyingly assured conviction, that she would inevitably become his mistress.

'Heavens, Jill, as you're the only friend I have, the least I expected was a bit of sympathy, not shrieks of laughter,' she complained to her convulsed assistant.

'I'm sorry, Cassie,' choked Jill. 'But I can't stop imagining the expression on Sacha's face when he walked in there... and when your ghastly landlady accosted you both!'

'But you can see that I had no alternative but to take up his offer?' she pleaded. 'If I'm to continue sending the amount I promised Helen, I can't pay rent without taking on a second job——'

'And Sacha's ruled that out,' cut in Jill, sobering completely. 'Of course I can see that, Cassie. But have you considered telling him the truth?' she added quietly.

'No, I can't—that's completely out of the question,' blurted out Cassandra, her heart sinking as she saw Jill's puzzled reaction to her vehemence. 'And now for a real laugh,' she continued hastily, determined to side-track Jill. 'The reason Sacha wants me in his office by eleven.'

'Which is in ten minutes' time,' pointed out Jill.

But by the time Cassandra had finished her hurried explanation Jill hadn't laughed once and her expression had become one of brooding concern.

'Cassie, all this interest Sacha takes in you goes far beyond that of an employer for an employee,' she sighed.

'And, once he really decides to turn on the charm, you won't stand a chance...'

'One thing I'll give you,' conceded Sacha humourlessly, as they entered the house with their arms laden, 'is that you certainly differ from other women in your complete indifference to your appearance.'

Cassandra hurled the mountain of bags she was carrying to the floor. She had spent the best part of the day suffering humiliation at his hands, and she was utterly exhausted.

'That's just where you're wrong,' she rounded on him. 'I like beautiful clothes just as much as the next woman. But unlike the floosies you consort with, my interest stops far short of being carted around from place to place, branded in everyone's eyes as...as a...'

'Well, spit it out,' he drawled, opening his arms and scattering the rest of the packages at their feet.

'They must have thought I was some sort of beggar, picked off the streets by bloody Father Christmas!'

'Stop swearing, it doesn't suit you,' he scowled, 'and anyway, what was I supposed to do——?'

'You could at least have let me attempt to choose some of the things myself, instead of acting as though I were a mindless clothes-horse!'

'Considering the well-above-average salary you earn, I can't see what's stopped you indulging this alleged love of clothes of yours.' He suddenly clutched his head in a theatrical display of consternation. 'Forgive me—I forgot! You earn so little that you're forced to earn extra in a strip joint in order to buy your sister a birthday present.' His look switched to one of sneering contempt. 'And even when, in consideration of your obvious penury, I gave you one of my credit cards, all you could stir yourself to get was one solitary outfit!'

'That's all I——'

'And as for doing your own choosing today—as I remember, it was only after I'd threatened to join you in the changing-rooms that you deigned even to try anything on!'

With a defiant toss of her head, Cassandra squatted down and began piling up the strewn packages, doing so only because he had made a point with which she had no valid argument.

'And I don't know where you get this ludicrous idea that I get some sort of kick traipsing around shops with women and selecting their clothes for them—you are the first and, I hope to God, the last.' He stooped and picked up several of the bags. 'Now, let's get this lot up to your room.'

Cassandra picked up the rest and followed him up the stairs.

'By the way,' he called over his shoulder to her, 'I forgot to mention that we're meeting a few people for dinner this evening—I suggest the blue and green Liberty print as we shan't be going on anywhere after.'

'What time are we leaving?' she asked, able to ignore his high-handed suggestion as to what she should wear thanks to the odd feeling of relief she experienced at being called on to start fulfilling her part of the bargain.

'In a couple of hours, I'm afraid,' he apologised, following her into the bedroom and tipping the purchases on to the bed. 'Perhaps if you just had a quick shower, you could have half an hour's nap—you must be tired.'

'I'm OK,' she stated, feeling inexplicably awkward in the face of this unexpected concern. 'I'd better get these put away.'

He nodded, an unfamiliar uncertainty in his eyes before he strolled towards the door. He turned as he reached it.

'And you're wrong about the impression you feel we might have created this afternoon,' he said quietly. 'If it's any consolation, we probably came over as a married couple barely on speaking terms.'

He could hardly have been accused of turning on the charm, she thought miserably, remembering Jill's earlier words of warning as she began unpacking and putting away the clothes. But she hadn't stood a chance...she had never stood a chance with Sacha.

Soon she had both built-in whitewood wardrobes on either side of the dressing-table almost full. And as she hung up the last of the blouses her hand reached out and stroked the costly softness of the material. Though their price alone made them garments she would never normally even have looked at, she couldn't deny their perfection. And there wasn't a single item that didn't do a special something for her she would never have dreamed possible... His taste was faultless.

But was the fact that a man possessed exquisite taste reason enough to love him?

She gave an agitated shake of her head, then went to the bathroom and turned on the shower.

She might just as well pick on the fact that he had strong, even and dazzlingly white teeth...because there was no rational reason whatever why she should love him...but she did.

'Cassandra, I'm sorry—I should have realised how exhausted you'd be,' muttered Sacha, as he handed her into a taxi outside the restaurant they had just left. 'And we'd better get the doctor to have another look at the ankle of yours—you seem to have started limping again.'

'Sacha, I'm fine—honestly!' she exclaimed, feeling a twinge of guilt because she suspected he had terminated the evening early on her account.

There had been an air of remoteness about him the entire evening, yet the drawling cynicism with which he normally peppered his remarks had been curiously absent.

'I really liked the Denhams,' she blurted out, giving in to an inexplicable need to fill the silence between them. 'Moira Denham was one of my father's students at Cambridge ten years ago.'

'Moira's an extremely nice woman,' he said. 'What did you think of the Langtons?'

Cassandra felt herself stiffen. 'Bill Langton was very interesting to talk to,' she managed neutrally—but she suspected it was his wife's presence that had had much to do with Sacha's air of withdrawal all evening; the woman who had pointedly sung the seemingly ubiquitous Deborah's praises to her whenever an opportunity had arisen.

'Yes, I have quite a few business dealings with Bill—pity his wife's such a first-class bitch.' He paused, then added quietly, 'But I daresay you discovered that for yourself.'

She wondered how much of Honor Langton's disclosures he had overheard, an ache of savage intensity rekindling in her as she remembered the last of them. 'Poor Sacha, he's certainly learned the hard way that a man in love is wasting his time playing hard to get. Never mind, I'm sure we'll see a happy ending when Deborah puts him out of his misery and drops that rather naughty suit she brought against him...she only did it to jerk him to his senses, and she certainly seems to have succeeded.'

'All in all, you came through the evening with flying colours,' he remarked, scattering her wounding thoughts as the cab drew up outside the house.

He leapt out to pay the driver, and as she moved to follow him she found herself wondering how much longer it could go on—this terrible propensity her life had of lurching from bad to worse. It was bad enough loving a man who despised her, but knowing he loved someone else only served to make it that much worse.

'Would you like me to make you a hot drink?' he asked brusquely as he closed the door behind them. 'You look rather tired.'

At best, it had been a begrudging offer of kindness, but its effect on her was devastating. Unable to say a word, she pushed past him and raced up the stairs to her room. Struggling free of her elegant new coat, she flung herself face down on the bed, channelling every shred of concentration she had in an attempt to dam the misery threatening to engulf her.

'Cassandra, what the hell's got into you?' he demanded, flinging open the door and storming into the room.

She tensed to breaking-point as the mattress gave slightly under his sudden weight.

Cassandra!' He turned her, his arms rough as they half lifted her. 'Cassandra, I ... Hell, can't you see this is exactly what I'm trying to fight against doing?' he groaned, pulling her fully into his arms and holding her suffocatingly close.

'Why?' she choked, her body lifeless against his despite the treacherous warmth already stealing through her. 'You've already made it plain you know all you have to do is snap your fingers and I'm yours!'

'Has it never occurred to you to wonder what would happen if you were to snap your fingers?' he demanded harshly. 'Do you think I enjoy being driven by a need I find almost impossible to rationalise? A need that simmers beneath the surface of my every waking moment?' He dropped his head to hers, his chin abrasive against her cheek as his lips murmured hotly against her temple. 'Yes, I do know you want me, but that's all I know. No matter how experienced you may be, how can I be sure I wouldn't frighten or even hurt you were I to drop my guard completely?'

'Sacha——' She lifted her head, searching for words that refused to come. Then she reached up and stroked back the dark hair that had tumbled forward across his forehead, her unconscious action an unspoken acceptance of the love she bore him and its every consequence.

'You're sure?' he whispered hoarsely, his arms tightening fiercely as her lips gave their answer, then parted to the passionate onslaught of his.

There was a trembling gentleness in the hands that undressed her, but it was only when he had shed his own clothes and drawn her shivering body to the turgid heat of his that the spectre of fear drifted through the wings of her mind. But it was the delicate sureness in those hands that drove her to an aching madness of need that kept her fear at bay, disguising its presence while the need grew in her until it brought his name sobbing from her lips in a fevered plea. Yet it was the sound of her own cries that ultimately rekindled the fear in her, fanning it to a surge almost of panic, even as she clung to him in desperate denial of it.

'Cassandra,' he groaned raggedly against her mouth, his entire body tensing, 'I can feel the fear in you even now.'

'No!' she cried, the savage need in her superseding all else as her body moved in blatant demand against his. 'How could I ever be afraid of wanting you like this?'

Her name whispered on his lips in answer to her words, and then there was only one brief moment of recoil to cast doubt on her impassioned claim before her body arched in joyous welcome to the total invasion of his.

And in the tempestuous arms of the man she so loved, she learned every answer to the needs he had awoken in her. And with each miraculous answer came the sharing of an ecstasy so intense that, when its final explosion came it came in a million fragments of effervescing delight, each fragment dancing through her in joyous abandon until they danced themselves to exhaustion and slipped from her lips in soft sighs of dazed and incredulous laughter.

CHAPTER EIGHT

EVEN in sleep there was a remarkable vibrancy in the relaxed features over which the pale wintry light of morning delicately crept. Cassandra's eyes lingered with love on the tanned breadth of shoulders, moving downwards to the matted darkness of hair on Sacha's chest that ended abruptly where the covers began.

Perhaps beauty was only in the eye of the beholder, she thought with dreamy wonderment, but what eye could be blind to the physical beauty of this man sleeping beside her?

There could certainly be no going back now, she reminded herself unnecessarily, and found herself responding to that knowledge, not with apprehensive fear, but with a stomach-churning intensity of excitement as she remembered the uninhibited frenzy with which that sleeping body had goaded hers to pleasures unimagined.

She raised exploratory fingers to her own passion-bruised lips and knew there was no part of her untouched by the tempestuous ardour that had invaded her.

She gave a small start as his eyes opened, bluer than she had ever known them. Then a breathless stillness took possession of her as she awaited his first words.

'If I had the energy, I'd be giving you the verbal blasting of your life.'

The tight knot of fearful anticipation in her unravelled with spontaneous relief. There had been an underlying caress in those huskily murmured words, just as there was open caress in the hand now reaching out and exploring the telltale rigidity that peaked her left breast.

It registered somewhere in a remote part of her that perhaps she should be examining those soft words, but all she could do was gaze down at those teasing, caressing fingers and marvel at the chaotic excitement they were wreaking on her every sense.

'Cassandra, I told you of the fears I had about losing control,' he chided gently.

'But you neither hurt nor frightened me,' she protested breathlessly, her eyes refusing to meet his.

'That doesn't alter the fact that I was completely out of control...and with a totally inexperienced virgin.' With a sigh of exasperation, he drew her down against him. 'And don't try telling me you didn't lie to me—because you near as damn it did by implication.'

She nestled against him, examining this curious ease she was feeling, despite his accusation. 'I know I did... It's just that I got fed up with being regarded as some sort of freak when I admitted the truth.'

He gave a soft chuckle. 'I'm still in two minds as to whether I should be thanking my stars or cursing them!'

'I think you should be thanking them,' she murmured, unquestioningly accepting the inexplicable feeling of contentment seeping through her.

'Really?' he chuckled, his tightening arms swiftly rekindling the sweet sharpness of longing in her.

Her mouth had just begun exploring against his shoulder when she suddenly sat up, her face a picture of childlike disappointment.

'Mrs E will be here any minute!' she wailed.

'Oh, dear...are you very disappointed, Cassandra?' he murmured, laughing as he cupped her suddenly blushing face in his hands. 'Perhaps I should have told you,' he whispered huskily, a languorous darkness creeping into his eyes. 'Mrs E doesn't come in at the weekends.'

'Cassie, for heaven's sake, you've got to ease up a bit,' protested Jill. 'All this tightening up on organisation you've been doing—it's—it's getting to the stage when we'll be drawing up lists of lists!'

'I want the Tower to be running as smoothly as it did under Alexander Carmichael by the time Harold Millar comes in to take over,' said Cassandra defensively.

'Cassie, it's months before he arrives!' exclaimed Jill. 'And how much more smoothly can a place run? I'm beginning to feel like a robot!'

'Jill, I'm sorry—I just didn't think,' sighed Cassandra, her face tense and strained as she sank down on the chair at her desk.

'Cassie, are you trying to prove something to Sacha?' demanded Jill quietly.

Was she? wondered Cassandra wearily. Intense and seemingly unquenchable though their shared passion was, it also brought with it a relaxed closeness that made Sacha's abrupt and inevitable switches back to remote coldness all the more unbearable. Was she trying to prove to him that she too could be a warm, uninhibited lover by night and a coldly efficient robot by day?

'Cassie, you haven't been reading all that drivel that's been in the papers recently?' exclaimed Jill, and would have given anything to take back those rash words when she saw Cassandra's puzzled frown.

'If you mean that Deborah Willis is back in circu-lation,' said Cassandra, realisation suddenly coming to her, 'I could hardly be ignorant of the fact with Lisa and her cronies talking of nothing else whenever I'm around.' A terrible fear began permeating her as one look at Jill's face told her that wasn't what she had meant. 'So, what's been in the papers?'

Jill tried a dismissive shrug, which didn't come off.

'Jill, if you have a paper with something in it, I'd like to see it,' Cassandra told her in a deathly quiet voice.

With obvious reluctance, the girl went to her office and returned with a folded paper.

'It's only what gossip columnists are saying…and even you must know how inventive they can be,' muttered Jill, a note almost of pleading in her voice as she handed over the paper.

The headline, written in bold print above a photograph, read, 'A happy ending after all?' There was no discernible expression on Sacha's unsmiling face, but there was laughter and vivacious confidence on that of the slim, dark-haired and breathtakingly lovely woman by his side.

As she read on, Cassandra learned several things, all hitherto unknown, about Deborah Willis: that she was American and a successful novelist, and had very recently decided to drop the breach of contract suit she had taken against the man at her side. The jokey words of the columnist echoed Honor Langton's words of three weeks before—that Deborah's plainly calculated action had seemed to have had its desired effect.

Cassandra let the paper fall to her desktop.

'So?' she asked, that one toneless word masking all those nameless fears so long suppressed and now leaping unfettered to the surface.

'Precisely—so!' stated Jill firmly. 'We'll start with Lisa and that wretched clone of hers, Amanda. The reason for their open bitchiness to you is plain jealousy.' Refusing to acknowledge Cassandra's look of open disbelief, she continued, 'Can't you see that they'd both quite happily sell their souls just to be able to bring the look on to Sacha's face that you do whenever you enter a room?'

'It's called lust,' snapped Cassandra in an explosion of pent-up bitterness, surprised to learn that Jill had ever seen such a look. Before, during and after their love-making were the only times Sacha normally let his guard down. It was at those other times when his undisguised resentment of his insatiable need for her spilled over in cutting sarcasm, negating every moment of gentleness and passion they had shared...until the next time. An unending roller-coaster of joy and despair from which there was no escape.

'Cassandra, are you really that blind?' whispered Jill, plainly shocked.

'No, I'm not blind,' replied Cassandra, her words hollow with despair. 'One thing I can honestly say is that my eyes have been wide open from the start.'

She had survived the past three weeks living only from moment to moment, taking the magic and closing her mind to the reality of everything else...because that was the only possible way for her to survive.

'But Sacha's eyes haven't,' Jill stated bluntly. 'Because you still refuse to tell him the truth.' She hesitated, taking a deep breath before she continued. 'Cassie, the other day when Elaine showed the three of us those carvings her brother had made—it was obvious you were really taken by one in particular. And it was just as ob-

vious that Sacha was about to buy it for you ... and that
something suddenly held him back.'

'I know...he was waiting to see if I'd buy it for myself,'
agreed Cassandra miserably. 'He's almost paranoid
about my not spending money... But if there was a time
I could have told him, it was the day he first interviewed
me. There's no way I could ever tell him now.'

'Hang on, I'd better get that,' muttered Jill apologetically as the phone rang in her office.

Cassandra nodded abstractedly, lost in thought.

'I'm afraid I'm wanted over in Personnel,' Jill called
out to her a few moments later.

Cassandra placed her elbows on the desk, cupping her
chin in her hands as she faced the fact that she was now
alone with thoughts she could no longer avoid.

Though Sacha's going out on his own on three sep-
arate evenings in just over a week had brought it home
to her just how fragile and undefined their relationship
was—she had felt unable, even for casual interest's sake,
to enquire where he was going—she had not felt in the
least threatened. But threatening was too mild a word
to describe what realising he had been with Deborah was
doing to her—jagged knives of despair were slicing
through her.

And last night, the first in which he hadn't come to
her, and during which she had spent the last few hours
of her birthday alone ... had he spent those hours in the
arms of the woman so many seemed certain he loved?

She reached out automatically as the phone on her
desk rang.

'Cassandra? Sacha—I'll see you in the foyer in a
couple of minutes.'

'Yes,' she replied, uncertainty in her tone.

'We're lunching with that advertising chap I told you about, and his wife—had you forgotten?'

'No, I just hadn't realised the time,' she said. 'I'll see you in the foyer.'

He was standing, slouched almost, against the main reception desk when she stepped out of the lift, and she found herself wondering, as she had so often recently, if the time would ever come when her senses no longer leapt in such wild tumult at the mere sight of him.

He straightened when he caught sight of her. 'Cassandra, you don't happen to have a couple of aspirins on you, do you?' he asked, taking her by the arm and steering her towards the outer doors. 'My head's about to explode.'

'I'm afraid I haven't,' she informed him, adding unkindly, 'That's certainly some hangover you have!'

That morning he had rounded on her sharply over breakfast for conducting a conversation from the dining-room with Mrs E, who had been in the kitchen. Seconds later he had excused his surliness by pleading a hangover. Even then Cassandra had had a few doubts about his claim—he drank very little. Now she found herself bitterly wondering just how much his outing the night before with Deborah had to do with his foul morning temper. Though he did look a bit rough, she thought, as he climbed into the driving seat next to her.

Angrily suppressing any feelings of anxiety over his appearance, she reminded herself that any complications in his relationship with the wretched Deborah were probably of his own making—by all accounts, Deborah Willis could hardly be accused of playing hard to get.

'Damn it, we're right out of petrol!' he exclaimed exasperatedly, a few minutes later. 'We'll have to backtrack as there isn't a garage between here and the restaurant.'

Cassandra found herself almost wishing for the distraction of running out of petrol completely as her mind perversely became filled with images of Deborah in his arms. By the time they had drawn into a petrol station and he was filling up the car, her mind had got around to the even more painful occupation of wondering just what it would be like to have Sacha's love.

She glared at his retreating back as he went into the station to pay, then frowned as he almost instantly reappeared.

'I've left my damned wallet somewhere,' he exclaimed, as she rolled down her window to find out what was wrong. 'Would you write out a cheque for me?'

'I haven't my cheque-book on me,' she muttered apologetically, annoyed to feel the colour rise in her cheeks.

'That credit card I gave you—use that.'

'I'm sorry... I haven't got that on me either,' she stammered.

'Great!' he fumed, throwing up his hands in disgust. 'You'd better ring Lisa while I have a word with someone here.' He put his hand in his pocket and pulled out a handful of change. 'I'd hate you to be out of pocket over a phone call,' he remarked scathingly as he handed her the money. 'Tell Lisa that if she can't find my wallet either in my overcoat or on my desk, to get hold of some cash and bring it here by taxi.'

Her cheeks scarlet, Cassandra selected two ten-pence pieces from among the coins; when she made to hand the rest back to him, he had gone.

She got out of the car and looked for a pay phone, a tight knot of misery and dejection bunching inside her.

The whole question of money—and Sacha's increasingly barbed references to it—was getting her down. Paying the extortionate advance on the room she had so briefly rented had left her overdrawn at the bank. Though she had promised the bank manager she would write no more cheques until the debt was cleared, last Saturday the milkman had called while Sacha was out and she had felt she had no option but to give him a cheque. She had also—and this time with trepidation, as the amount had staggered her—paid by cheque for some dry-cleaning of Sacha's Mrs E had asked her to collect.

Forcing such uncomfortable thoughts from her mind, she got through to the office and spoke to Lisa. She took a deep breath once she had finished—one thing was sure, she couldn't go on like this much longer. She had lost her heart, but soon she would have lost every last shred of her pride as well. Once Christmas was over, she would ring Helen and tell her the truth.

As she made her way back to the car, a sickening realisation pulled her up abruptly. It was madness to think she even had until after Christmas—Sacha and Deborah had obviously begun sorting out their relationship, probably had completely for all she knew . . . She had no time left at all.

'Lisa's on her way—she'd already found your wallet on your desk.'

'Get that, will you, Cassandra?' muttered Sacha wearily that evening, as the sound of the ringing phone greeted them as they entered the house.

Flashing an openly worried look at his flushed, drawn face, Cassandra picked up the phone in the hall.

'Mrs E!' she exclaimed, her surprise turning to concern as she listened to the housekeeper's croaking voice. 'You should have gone home the moment you started feeling bad... You just take care of yourself,' she soothed. 'And don't worry about a thing here—promise?'

She went into the sitting-room and found Sacha sprawled on the sofa, still in his overcoat.

'That was Mrs E—she's got a bad dose of the flu or something—she sounded ghastly.' Realisation suddenly dawned on her as she gazed down at the prone man. 'And I've a nasty suspicion you've got the same thing,' she sighed, dropping to her haunches beside the sofa. 'Sacha, why on earth did you tell me you had a hangover this morning?'

'Because it felt like one,' he growled.

'And what does it feel like now?' she demanded, reaching out to feel his forehead—it was burning.

'Just leave me alone and let me die in peace,' he protested, heaving himself over and presenting his back to her. 'What the hell are you doing?' he exclaimed suddenly.

'Removing your shoes before they mark the upholstery,' she replied. 'Sacha, don't you think you should at least take off your coat?'

'In a minute—just leave me alone,' he complained.

Trying, with little success, to convince herself that the chances of his dying of flu were virtually nil, Cassandra removed her own coat, then tore through the house in search of aspirins. She eventually found some in the bathroom adjoining his bedroom, then raced down the stairs to the kitchen.

She returned to the sitting-room seconds later, a glass containing dissolving aspirins clutched tightly in her noticeably shaking hand. She was behaving pathetically, she berated herself as she approached the apparently sleeping man—still clad in his bulky overcoat.

'Sacha, drink this—it's only a couple of aspirins, but it might help a little.'

With a muttered complaint he heaved himself over, took the glass, drained it and handed it back to her.

'Thanks,' he croaked. 'Just let me sleep for a while and I'll be fine.' He heaved himself back to his former position.

Cassandra was toying once more with suggesting that he remove his overcoat, when the phone rang.

'What number did you say?' demanded a startled, decidedly American female voice.

Cassandra repeated the number, an unpleasant sensation crawling over her skin as she did so.

'Who exactly are you, then?' the voice again demanded.

'I...I'm the housekeeper,' stammered Cassandra, immediately wanting to kick herself for so patently obvious a lie.

'Right—tell Mr Carmichael that Deborah Willis wishes to speak with him.'

'One moment, please,' Cassandra answered, with an efficiency that astounded her, given not only the drunken lurching taking place in the region of her stomach but her astonishment that her claim to be the housekeeper had gone unchallenged.

She returned to the sitting-room.

'Sacha.' She reached out and gently shook his shoulder when he made no reply. 'Sacha—Deborah Willis is on the phone, she wants to speak to you.'

'What about?'

Gritting her teeth with frustration, Cassandra marched back to the hall.

'I'm afraid Mr Carmichael's not very well at the moment,' she announced with false calm. 'Could I give him a message?'

The silence greeting her words became so prolonged that she was on the verge of repeating them when the woman eventually replied.

'Yes. Tell him this.' There was unadorned fury in the voice. 'Tell him I shan't be seeing him tonight...that I'm catching the nine-thirty flight back to New York.'

'If you'll hold on again for a moment, I'll tell him now,' offered Cassandra, but the woman had hung up before she had completed the sentence.

This was the last sort of thing she needed to be involved in, she raged, a mixture of hopelessness, fear and her first taste of the terrible sourness of jealousy churning biliously within her. Yet again she returned to the sitting-room, determined to get it over and done with before she was physically sick.

'She says she's catching the nine-thirty flight back to New York,' she blurted out. 'Sacha—did you hear what I said?' she shouted frustratedly at his motionless form.

'For God's sake! I heard—satisfied?' he bellowed, staggering to his feet. 'What does a man have to do to get a bit of peace and quiet around here?' he added, lurching unsteadily from the room.

Clamping her lips tightly shut, Cassandra stormed off to the kitchen. If he thought she was going to hang around and let him use her as some sort of glorified whipping-boy—and just because his ridiculous relationship with the obnoxious Deborah had taken another downturn—he had another thought coming. They obviously deserved one another!

Her furious thoughts ended abruptly as the automatic oven suddenly hummed to life. She took a peep inside,

her face softening when she saw that Mrs E had prepared a chicken casserole before finally staggering home
to her sick-bed.

She really would miss Mrs E, she thought sadly, as
she began preparing rice to go with the kindly housekeeper's dish. She glanced down at her watch, working
out what time it would be in Boston now. She would
ring Helen tonight and make a clean breast of everything to her.

Feeling, if anything, even worse than she had before
she had come to that decision, she began reciting 'The
Owl and the Pussy-Cat', her favourite childhood poem,
to herself to distract her thoughts as she made a side
salad to go with the meal.

'...they danced by the light of the moon, the moon.
They danced by the light of the moon.'

She knocked a serving spoon from the table as she
spun round in shock.

'Sacha! You gave me a fright!'

He was in a dressing-gown and pyjamas, and he looked
rumpled and drowsy and decidedly unwell.

'I'm sorry. And I'm sorry too for the unforgivable
way I snapped at you earlier... I realise it's no excuse,
but I feel pretty rough.'

'And you look it, Sacha!' she exclaimed. 'Mrs E's
made a chicken casserole—why don't you just go back
to bed and I'll bring you some later?'

'I'm thirsty,' he muttered, going to the fridge and
taking out some fresh orange juice. He drank two full
glasses and poured himself a third. 'Would you like
some?'

She shook her head, her eyes clouding with anxiety.

He made to sit down, then hesitated, glancing over at her. 'I suppose I'd better get out of here...you'll only catch my germs.'

'By now I'll already have caught any germs I'm likely to,' she pointed out gently.

'I suppose so,' he muttered uncertainly, then sat down.

'Are you hungry?' she asked, a powerful and completely non-sexual urge to put her arms around him gripping her.

'Not really. I forgot to tell Mrs E we'd be lunching out today...but I suppose that's just as well, as you didn't eat much lunch.'

'No—I didn't feel particularly hungry,' she replied, her tone constrained as her eyes suddenly dropped from his.

'Cassandra, why were you looking at me like that?' he asked.

'Like what?'

He shrugged, then picked up his glass and began drinking slowly from it.

Tonight she was ringing Helen, and soon all this would be over, she thought numbly. And though he would never know of the terrible strength of the love she would probably always feel for him, there was a yearning in her to feel, if only once, his arms around her and hers around him other than in the heat of passion.

She went to where he sat, then she placed her arms around his head and cradled it to her.

For an instant he tensed, then he relaxed completely against her.

'You're quite the little mother, deep down, are you?' he chuckled.

'I don't know about that,' she murmured, her hands stroking against his hair. 'I just don't like seeing you ill.'

'I can't say it's a bundle of laughs feeling it either. But I think it only fair to warn you I make a lousy patient, so you'd best steer clear of me while I'm like this.'

'Warning taken,' she murmured, an aching sadness of peace settling around her. 'Shall I light the sitting-room fire? You'd probably feel more comfortable in there.'

'We could curl up in front of it.'

She tilted his face—his words had been without any discernible expression. He smiled up at her lazily.

'See—no sarcasm intended,' he laughed, accurately interpreting her action. 'We can curl up on the sofa in front of the fire, while I seek your advice...and advice is something I'm sorely in need of.'

'Right, I'll call you when the fire's lit,' she said briskly, freeing him and racing to the sitting-room.

She knelt before the set fire, her breath coming in panting gulps as she lit it. He wouldn't...he couldn't!

The warmth where his head had rested still nuzzled against her midriff: hadn't he felt the loving spilling from her and over him?

She rose as the fire caught and rested her head against the cool marble of the mantelpiece. Night after night she had lain in his arms and given freely of her love...and now he was about to talk to her of love...his love for another woman.

'Cassandra, what's wrong?' He came to her side, his arm slipping across her shoulders. 'Hell, you're not coming down with this wretched bug too, are you?' he exclaimed with sympathetic anxiety.

'No, I...I got up a bit too quickly and felt a little giddy, that's all.'

'Come and sit down,' he urged, drawing her over to the sofa. 'I've turned the oven right down and put the rice in it too, so it should keep safely for a couple of hours or so.'

'I cooked the rice too soon,' she muttered distractedly. Any moment now he would start talking—asking for her advice—and any moment now, she knew without doubt, she was going to make a monumental fool of herself... Her every reserve of strength was used up.

And as he sat down on the sofa beside her the terrible irony of it all hit her with ferocious intensity—the one time he was displaying affection towards her in which sexual undertones played no part was the time he was about to break her heart irreparably.

'Cassandra, I need your honest opinion—no holds barred,' he stated, his fingers stroking absentmindedly against her painfully tensing shoulder. 'It's my brother Max—you remember I told you the saga of him and the older woman... Cassandra, you're shaking! You *have* got this damned bug!'

'No—I haven't,' she gasped, struggling for breath. 'I...I was about to sneeze...but it didn't come.'

He frowned, obviously not in the least convinced by her stammered words.

'You were saying about Max,' she prompted breathlessly, her spirits soaring as though she had been reprieved from a life sentence.

'Yes, well...it seems he's as serious as ever about this wretched woman. He's asked to bring her home for Christmas.'

Lightheaded with relief, she made an effort to compose herself. 'And you want my honest opinion?' she managed.

'Cassie, I'm desperate for it,' he pleaded.

It was the first time he had ever shortened her name, and it came like the softest of endearments to her ears.

'Well, the way I understand it, you obviously love your brother dearly and would hate there to be a permanent wedge between you both.'

'That would be unthinkable!'

'Yet you've judged as nothing more than a fortune-hunter the woman he says he loves—even though you've never even met her. Sacha, has their age difference really anything to do with your negative reaction—or is it the mere fact that he's involved with any woman?'

'I'd hardly be over the moon if it were another man he was involved with,' he snapped. 'He's so young—only a year younger than you are, for heaven's sake!'

'Two—I'm twenty-four.' It was a silly remark to have made, but it had slipped out almost of its own volition. 'Anyway,' she added hastily, hoping it hadn't registered with him, 'you haven't really much choice, other than to tell him he's welcome to bring her home for Christmas. Then you'll just have to make a concerted effort to rid your mind of all its totally unjustified prejudices and judge her on her own merits.'

'Quite the wise little owl, aren't you?' he sighed. 'And of course you're right.' He stretched back his head and flexed his shoulder muscles. 'Do you mind if I lie down?' he asked. 'This bloody headache seems to be coming back.'

He arranged himself on the sofa, stretching out with his head on her lap.

'I'll write to Max tomorrow and tell him they're both welcome here for Christmas,' he muttered. 'I know I've gone overboard with this heavy-handed father routine, but despite the age difference between us we've always been very close. And probably because of the age difference I've felt some sort of obligation to adopt the role of father in this particular instance... Not that it's come in the least easily, as you've no doubt gathered,' he finished with a wry laugh.

'And I've also gathered how much you love him,' she murmured, her fingers massaging gently against his temples. 'How's the head?'

'So-so,' he replied drowsily. 'But that feels good.'

He slept for over an hour, and as she gazed down at his sleeping face her own was bathed in the soft glow of love and she knew that this moment, above any other, would become engraved on her heart as one of the happiest of her life.

Her face suddenly clouded as she examined that realisation. It didn't say much for the quality of her life, she reflected bitterly, if her happiest moment was to be that spent with a man whose interest in her was almost exclusively sexual, and whose volatile love was for a woman as beautiful and sophisticated and as far removed from her as he.

Though this evening's interlude was one she would always treasure, it made no iota of difference to the facts. And the facts were something she would have to face squarely—starting with her call to Helen later.

He awoke flushed and heavy-eyed.

'When were you twenty-four?' he demanded sleepily.

'Yesterday,' she replied—it no longer mattered.

'And you were all alone,' he sighed in that same sleep-laden voice. 'I wanted you last night—just as I always want you...I wish I'd come to you.'

'Why—because it happened to be my birthday?'

'Perhaps... I've discovered it's not always that simple, having a relationship as singularly sexual as ours. There are times I want you so badly it's like an ache within me...yet I suppress it because...'

For a moment she was almost certain he had drifted back into sleep.

'Though I don't know why I sometimes have a need to hide what I'm feeling from you, because although in most exclusively sexual relationships there's usually a dominant partner, most often the man, it's never been like that with us... Is that as confusing to you as it sounded to me, or do you understand what I'm trying to say?'

'If you're saying I shouldn't feel that you've used me, I don't...and I never have,' she told him quietly.

And it was true, she realised. In that one contentious area where her self-esteem should have been at its most vulnerable, it never had been. Where her inability to tell him the truth and the consequent confrontations over her lack of money were concerned, her self-esteem had been whittled away. But never where their lovemaking was involved; there they met always as true equals, each giving unstintingly to the other and nothing—oddly enough, not even his love for another woman—could ever take that away from her.

But one thing she would never understand was how he could love one woman and need another as he needed her... The male psyche was one she would never be able to understand in a million years, she thought bemusedly.

'Perhaps that was what I was saying...but I'm sorry to have missed your birthday. Why didn't you tell me?'

She gave a small shrug. 'It didn't seem that important. Sacha, are you hungry?'

He shook his head. 'If you don't mind, I think I'd better haul myself back to bed.'

'I'll make you up a hot toddy, if you like.'

'I'd like,' he murmured, rising.

'Sacha, would you mind if I rang my sister later?'

'Be my guest...Cassie, you don't have to ask my permission to use the phone.'

CHAPTER NINE

'HELEN? It's Cassie!'

'Oh, Cassie, it's so good to hear your voice!'

Cassandra suddenly tensed sharply.

'Cassie, I wanted to ring you yesterday for your birthday, but you know how it is, and anyway I haven't got your new number——'

'Helen, you're crying—what's wrong?' exclaimed Cassandra, her expression filled with alarm and fear.

'Nothing...it's just so good to hear you,' choked Helen.

'Helen, you know that won't wash with me,' protested Cassandra, her own voice threatening to break.

'I'm just feeling a bit low,' replied Helen, the effort she was making to control herself apparent despite the miles separating them. 'And anyway, time's too precious to waste discussing my moodiness—how are you, darling? Did you have a good birthday?'

'Helen, time isn't a problem with this call, and you're the least moody person I know,' persisted Cassandra. 'Is it Charles?' she asked with a sickening flash of inspiration when her sister made no reply.

She felt the tears streaming down her own cheeks as she heard Helen's stifled sob.

'He asked me to marry him... He says he's never stopped loving me... All those years, and he never stopped,' sobbed Helen.

'Oh, Helen . . . if only I could be with you,' murmured Cassandra brokenly. She had never known her sister be in a state like this before. 'Did you tell him about Dad?'

'How could I, Cassie? He's not one of those doctors who thinks in terms of how much money they can earn—he does most of his work with the poor.'

'But Dad's debt is ours,' protested Cassandra. 'He wouldn't have to be involved in it at all.'

'He's the sort of man who'd involve himself anyway,' said Helen. 'And he's so dedicated to his work . . . I just couldn't bear the thought of him feeling obliged to go into a more lucrative practice just to help me.'

'And you think that's how he'd react?'

'I know it is,' sobbed Helen.

'So what did you say to him—when he asked you to marry him?'

'I told him I couldn't see him any more.'

'Helen, you love him!' protested Cassandra. 'You've loved him for as long as he's loved you!'

'Yes . . . and he asked me to tell him I didn't . . . and I couldn't bring myself to.'

'Oh, Helen,' whispered Cassandra, a terrible hopelessness washing over her.

'Cassie, how are things with you?' asked Helen, a brittle sadness colouring her words. 'For weeks now your letters have been . . . I don't know, perhaps rather like mine, in that they seem to be hiding all the things we daren't say.'

'I'm fine—really I am, Helen.'

'This Sacha—do you love him?'

Cassandra knew she had paused far too long before replying. 'Yes.'

'I'll say a prayer for you, Cassie,' Helen promised sadly. 'Say one for me too, won't you?'

When Cassandra replaced the receiver, a long shuddering sob broke from her as she buried her face in her hands.

Later she went to the kitchen and splashed her face with cold water as she waited for the kettle to boil.

And as she climbed the stairs with a steaming mug in her hand it occurred to her that none of the things she had intended telling Helen had been told. Then she tapped softly on the door of Sacha's room.

The bedside light was on and he stirred as she entered.

'I thought you might like another hot toddy,' she whispered, leaning down to feel his head as he turned heavy-lidded eyes towards her. 'You're very hot again, but the aspirin in the drink should help.'

She watched as he drank from the mug, her eyes anxious as they saw the lethargic slowness of his every movement.

'Can I get you anything else?'

'Are you positive you've already caught any germs you're likely to?' he mumbled thickly.

'Positive.'

He finished the drink, shivering slightly as he returned the mug to her.

'Well, there is one thing I'd like.'

'And what's that?'

'A Cassandra-shaped hot-water bottle for a while—I'm frozen.'

She gave a soft laugh, then climbed into the bed beside him.

'For how long would you like this hot-water bottle?' she murmured, reaching out and turning off the light.

He rolled on to his stomach, nestling his head into the hollow of her neck as his arm slipped around her and his hand cupped the curve of her shoulder.

'Probably forever,' he sighed sleepily.

'It's only a minor bout of flu and I'll probably have slept it off by this evening,' Sacha had croaked dismissively the next morning when she had pleaded with him to let her call in the doctor.

She had arrived at work late, taking with her for posting the letter he had insisted on writing to his brother before she had left; and she had left work early. And again that night they had slept in the platonic embrace of one another's arms.

On the third day, he was greatly improved, cooking her a meal that evening that had justified Mrs E's every claim regarding his culinary abilities. And that night had brought a reawakening of the passion between them, when the urgency of his ardour had broken down her last restraint and the words of love had poured from her in a soft, incoherent chant.

'Sacha, you should at least give yourself another day at home,' she protested on the fourth morning, when he announced that he was returning to work.

'Why?' he asked, a mischievous teasing in his eyes. 'So that I can rest up for another marathon like last night's?'

He chuckled softly as her colour deepened, and it was the sudden memory of her involuntary words of love that caused it to deepen even more.

'And well you might blush, young lady,' he murmured, his teasing lightheartedness confirming her feeling—more a fervent prayer—that perhaps he hadn't heard the actual words which had comprised her passionate outpouring.

'I do hope Mrs E's feeling better,' she told him as they left. 'I didn't like ringing in case I disturbed her.'

'I'll send her some flowers today,' he said, then stopped to take a bundle of post from the approaching postman.

Cassandra made a mental note to visit the Maltons again and collect any post they might have for her; Helen was the only person to whom she had given her new address, but then her sister was the only person likely to be writing to her.

She was conscious of how much more relaxed their journey to the office was than any other she could re-member. And when they parted in the foyer he hesi-tated, almost as though he was about to take her in his arms.

It had been a ludicrous flight of fancy on her part, she tried reasoning with herself as she made her way to her office... but for the rest of the day she walked on air.

The man from whom she had parted that morning was one still softened and gentled by the closeness his brief illness had created between them.

But the man with whom she travelled home that night had reverted to an edgy remoteness, the callous abruptness of which hurtled her back into that dark abyss of despair from which only her propensity for self-delusion had given her such brief respite.

'What would you like for supper this evening?' she asked, finally driven to break the leaden silence between them.

'Nothing,' he replied. 'One of the girls in Personnel had a birthday today, and I haven't yet recovered from the cakes she brought in. Did you sample one of them?'

'No—the Tower doesn't really get involved in events like that with the rest of the company.'

'Just as well—it must have cost that poor kid a fortune providing all those cakes,' he observed, his tone oddly chilling. 'Though I suppose on a bad day there could be quite a tidy number to cater for in the Tower, if you had all the eggheads in at one go working on their various projects. Was there a full complement around on your birthday the other day—or were you lucky?'

How glibly he had done it, thought Cassandra as she felt the sickening knotting-up sensation in her stomach, introducing that most contentious of all subjects—her finances.

'I told you—I didn't consider my birthday worth bothering about,' she stated defensively when he glanced at her with a look of pointed enquiry.

'I really must settle up what I owe you,' he murmured silkily, as they drew up in front of the house.

'You owe me nothing!' she exclaimed, wondering with sick desperation why he should be so deliberately spoiling for a fight.

He reached the front door just as she did.

'But I *must* owe you something,' he protested in a parody of innocence, inserting his key in the lock before she could use hers. 'For instance, there was that letter you posted for me the other day, and good heavens, we both know how extortionate postal charges are——'

'Sacha, why don't you just come out with it and say what you really mean?' she rounded on him, humiliation goading her to retaliate.

His eyes swept coldly over her as he removed his coat, then hung it up. 'My, my, Cassandra, that sounds suspiciously as though you're demanding honesty of me,' he drawled softly.

'I am,' she retorted recklessly, then clutched to her the coat she had just removed when she saw the sudden look of rage flash across his features.

'Oh, you are, are you?' he whispered, stepping towards her, the fury once more flashing in him as she automatically stepped back from him. 'Cassandra, would you for God's sake hang up that bloody coat, instead of clutching it to you like some sort of icon to ward off evil spirits!' he rasped.

She draped the coat over the banister, considering the carved wood coat-stand too close to her adversary for comfort.

'So—where were we? Ah, yes, *you* were demanding honesty from *me*.'

'Sacha, I know you might think I haven't perhaps been honest with you——'

'Really?' he cut in venomously. 'What an unfortunate sense of timing you have, my dear! Though I have to admit that if it weren't for that you might just have a great little act going for you there... not that there's any chance of it working on me, Cassandra—definitely not on me!'

He strode off into the sitting-room, leaving her ashen-faced and numbed with disbelief.

He made her feel like a criminal, she thought, frustration and humiliation welling up in her, while at the same time making it almost impossible for her even to attempt telling him the truth.

Her face flushed with anger, she followed him. 'Sacha, why do you seem to find it virtually impossible to regard women other than as part of some conspiracy to part you from your wretched money?' she demanded hotly.

'If you have as much of it as I have, it's a knack you learn pretty young,' he retorted dismissively. 'But of course, it's only a figment of my imagination that you haven't been completely honest with me about your finances, isn't it, Cassandra?' he went on, his tone now wheedling, though his face was completely without expression as he approached her and placed both hands lightly on her shoulders. 'Isn't it, Cassandra?' he repeated, his hands tightening as she refused to meet his gaze. 'So why don't you just look me in the eye and tell me how insignificant a part money plays in your life?'

'I certainly wouldn't choose to let it rule my life the way it obviously does yours!' she retorted, flinching as he jerked her a fraction closer to him.

'Surprise, surprise,' he taunted softly. 'And now I suppose you'll remind me of that little cash-flow problem you had, brought about by your having to fork out advance rent on the charming little place from which I lured you. Unfortunately you seem to have forgotten that I'm the one paying you a salary way above the expectations of anyone of your age and lack of experience. And also that the salary cheque you've since received should have more than straightened out that little problem ... unless, of course, you were already up to your pretty little eyeballs in debt to begin with ... Silly me, of course you weren't.'

She turned her face from his, hot colour staining her cheeks.

'Tell me, Cassandra, was it because you find me so utterly irresistible that you accepted my invitation to stay here?'

'This is the last place on earth I'd stay if I had the choice!' she flared, the words leaping from the depths of her humiliation.

'But how fortunate you were, having no choice yet finding a man who so neatly fulfilled your every requirement...one who couldn't keep his hands off you and one who, above all, had the necessary money. What I find so puzzling about it all is trying to work out when, exactly, you intended coming clean with me about precisely what it is you require from me.'

'I don't want anything from you,' she protested despairingly.

'Oh, but you do, Cassandra,' he taunted, pulling her sharply against him. 'Your body wants mine, just as it always has...and just as mine has always wanted yours. Was that what you were banking on—that my need of your body would ensnare me into loving you?' He gave a soft laugh. 'But surely you've done your homework on me—surely you've read all those informative little snippets appearing in certain types of papers during the past couple of weeks, telling you of my love for Deborah and the likelihood of my marrying her?'

It was the fact that he was stripping almost the last vestiges of her pride from her that paradoxically restored a measure of it to her. She placed her hands against his chest, forcing a space between their tensed bodies as her eyes squarely met the glittering contempt in his.

'You can say and think what you like, but nothing will ever alter the fact that I want no more from you than you've already given me,' she told him in a quiet, almost controlled voice. 'You asked me to fulfil certain duties as hostess in return for staying here and, in my ignorance, I agreed——'

'Your ignorance?' he echoed. 'The arrangement still stands—the agreement was that I would be the one terminating it. I still need a hostess and you still need a roof over your head.'

'If you need a hostess, I suggest you tell Deborah.'

'Deborah happens to be in the States.'

'Try snapping your fingers, Sacha,' she retorted recklessly. 'I'm sure she'd coming running back!'

'Cassandra, you sound almost jealous,' he mocked.

'Do I?' she spat, mortified by the inescapable truth
of his taunt.

'Yes...you do,' he murmured, drawing her slowly
towards him. 'And don't freeze as though you were about
to spurn my advances, Cassandra,' he coaxed, the
softness of his breath against her hair. 'Because you
know you never will.'

Her arms remained rigid at her sides, her hands
clenching to fists as he took her fully into his arms.

He lowered his head, his hair rustling against her chin
as his lips teased against her throat.

'Your pulses are racing, Cassandra,' he taunted, his
words a hot moistness against her skin. 'Just as they
always do.'

While one hand slid sensuously up her back, its fingers
twining into her hair, the other deftly coaxed undone
the buttons of her blouse. And though a soft, involuntary moan of pleasure sighed from her as his hands
then lightly cupped her breasts, her own hands remained
reluctant, unmoving fists. And even when the teasing
touch of his fingers through the flimsy fabric of her bra
sent ungovernable shivers of need rippling through her,
her arms remained rigid.

'Cassandra, you'll drive us both mad,' he breathed
unsteadily, his head lowering further till his lips were
nuzzling demandingly against the taut swell of her flesh
above her bra.

She gazed down at that dark beloved head nestled
against her and felt the sharpness of her nails biting into

the flesh of her palms as she fought the battle she could never win.

'Why pretend, Cassandra, when your body is so blatantly telling me all I need to know?' he pleaded huskily, straightening as his arms tightened fiercely around her to mould her wildly trembling body to the urgent proclamation of his own consuming need.

She closed her eyes, her arms and her body aching to break free and become lost in the magic of his.

Suddenly he placed his hands to her hips, drawing her from him as his head dropped to her shoulder, his breathing harsh and uneven.

'I suppose that wasn't the brightest of moves on my part, trying to turn sex against you,' he muttered hoarsely. 'And perhaps more because it was the single honest thing between us than because of my own conspicuous vulnerability in that area.' His hands slid to the small of her back, though he made no attempt to draw her to him again. 'And it was the one area in which we were completely honest with one another, wasn't it, Cassandra?'

She nodded, unable to trust herself to speak.

'Until you spoiled it last night by telling me you loved me,' he rounded on her harshly, his words uttering their rejection even as his arms pulled her fiercely to him once more.

'Did I?' she choked, words of outright denial refusing to come. 'I don't know what I'm saying when I'm in your arms.' Again she had tried and again the words had refused to come, and then, because it was the only way she could silence the love within her crying out to be reiterated, she placed her arms around him and buried her face against his chest.

And it was only the bruising hunger of his mouth, as it found hers, that silenced those words still begging their freedom.

'Love me, Cassandra,' he demanded, his hands impatient as they almost tore her clothes from her. 'Love me,' he repeated with hoarse urgency, excitement shuddering through him as her hands began responding with the same trembling impatience as his.

He lowered her to the patterned softness of the Persian rug before the hearth, his body fusing with hers in savage exultation as he answered the sobbed repetition of his own pleas now crying in his ears.

And later, when ecstasy had spent itself into soft tremors of contentment, they lay locked and glistening in one another's arms and she pressed her lips to his throat, savouring the sharp tang of his skin against her tongue while she silently chanted her vow of love.

Then her silent litany was interrupted by his soft, throaty chuckle, and the slow, sensuous throb of fire began lazily rekindling in her as he lifted her in his arms. And his laughter was a soft caress against her ears as he negotiated the discarded clothing littering his path, then carried her up the stairs to his room.

Deep down there was a consciousness in her of the spectre of a terrible desperation behind the frenzied inhibition of their lovemaking. And deep down, too, was her realisation that they were both being driven by their unacknowledged acceptance of how little time they had left before reality finally severed this sweet bond of madness enslaving them.

'Cassandra, we can exhaust our way into the record books till we drop, but it won't change the fact that a time must come when we'll have to talk,' he murmured against her, at a moment when she had been certain he was asleep.

'Except that you and I aren't able to talk,' she whispered defeatedly, turning her head from him as her mind became filled with strident memories of his accusation and contempt. 'Why can't you just accept that I don't want any of your money?' she pleaded.

'And why can't you just admit that it's my money that would solve whatever problem it is you have?' he demanded wearily.

'You're wrong,' she sighed, even now a trembling wonderment in her fingers as they softly traced the muscled curve of his back. 'Not even every penny you possess could do anything to solve my problem.'

And she knew she had spoken only the truth. What she had once regarded as an almost insurmountable problem no longer appeared that daunting. Whether it took one or fifty years to repay her father's debt, it would one day be behind her, but her heart was lost to her for eternity.

'So you're telling me I couldn't help even if I wanted to?'

'No, Sacha . . . not even if you wanted to.'

He had admitted his love for Deborah, she remembered numbly, and tonight, whether consciously or not, he was bidding his farewell to her and to the inexplicable magic in which he had become so reluctantly entrapped.

The next morning he was pale and heavy-eyed with exhaustion, a look Cassandra saw reflected in her own face in the bathroom mirror. And, though they exchanged few words over the breakfast he had silently prepared for them, it was a silence that held few of the charged undertones that had so demoralised her the previous morning. Not that her mental processes would have been up to registering it had he chosen to stand on the dining-room table and harangue her for thirty minutes, she pointed out to herself later in her office while the hours dawdled by without her having completed either a single task or thought a concrete thought.

She reached out lethargically as the phone rang.

'Sacha here.'

It was the same voice, yet one so different from that which had cried out time and again in passion to her throughout their torrid night, but it still had the power to rip open the wound of love that ached non-stop within her.

'I'm at the airport—I'm on my way to New York...Cassandra, are you still there?'

'I'm still here,' she echoed hollowly.

'I'm not sure how long I'll be gone—not that it appears to interest you greatly.'

The harshness, like an accusation, in his tone numbed her. What did he expect, she wondered bitterly, that she would go to pieces...beg him to stay?

'Should it?' she demanded, gripping the receiver with both hands as a terrible despair began shuddering through her.

'"Should" doesn't exactly come into it,' he retorted without expression. 'Just as it doesn't even come into why I'm taking this trip—but I am...so I'll be off.'

'Sacha, I...I wish you luck,' she whispered, words spoken from her heart. It was love that made it impossible for her to wish him anything other than happiness, despite its being someone other than herself with whom he would seek it.

'Do you, Cassie? Because I can tell you, I'm in sore need of some,' he replied quietly, then hung up.

She sat at her desk, staring unseeingly into space while the sound of her name on his lips filled her head... He had called her Cassie once more, and now of all times. Deep down she had known that last night had been his farewell to her... and now he was answering the call of love, thankful to be free from the tenuous bond that had once held him to her.

Her head lifted jerkily at the sound of the knock on her door, and her face was a pale mask of tension as she saw Lisa appear.

'I meant to pop round to see you earlier,' stated Lisa. 'But Sacha left me so many last-minute things to do when he suddenly took off—I've been running round in circles all afternoon.'

Cassandra watched the girl approach the desk, a detached feeling of other-worldliness settling on her as it occurred to her that this was the first time she could ever remember Lisa refer to Sacha by his first name.

'He's just rung me,' she heard herself say, her words sounding as peculiarly detached as her feelings.

'Cassandra, are you all right?'

'I'm fine,' she replied automatically, while another part of her detected something else she found a little odd: Lisa was sounding almost friendly. 'Did you want that report? I'm not sure if Jill's finished it yet.'

'No—she hasn't quite, but I can get it another time.' Lisa gave a tentative smile. 'Actually, Sacha asked me to give you this.' She handed Cassandra a large white envelope. 'Oh, and another thing—the girls in the main company usually go out for a meal in the week before Christmas—independent of the company do—and we wondered if you and Jill would like to join us?'

Cassandra's eyes widened slightly: she had no idea why, but Lisa was quite plainly holding out an olive

branch... and it would be churlish of her not to accept
it.

'That sounds lovely,' she said, smiling up at the girl.

'I'll give you plenty of warning once they've decided
on an actual date,' promised Lisa. 'I'm afraid I must be
off,' she added apologetically. 'I've still got one or two
things to finish off.'

'Talk about a transformation!' exclaimed Jill, breezing
in only moments after Lisa had left. 'Do you think
Sacha's had a go at her for being so snooty
towards——? Cassie?'

Cassandra looked up, her eyes dark with shock. Then
she returned them to the envelope she had moments
before opened. It was stuffed full of banknotes, and
clipped to one was a terse unsigned note, scrawled in
Sacha's distinctive hand.

'This should tide you over for any household expenses, et cetera, that might crop up.'

'Cassandra, what's wrong?' demanded Jill, alarm on
her face as she rushed to Cassandra's side and removed
the envelope from her rigid fingers. 'So... Sacha's left
you some housekeeping money,' she said quietly, tucking
the money and the note back into the envelope. 'Lisa
told me he's had to dash off somewhere
suddenly... Cassie?'

'He's gone to the States after Deborah. He's——'

'What do you mean—after Deborah?' snorted Jill
disbelievingly, seating herself on the desk-top.

'Exactly that—he loves her.'

'For heaven's sake, Cassie, only five minutes ago the
wretched woman was about to drag him through the
courts for breach of contract!'

'Jill, everyone knows it's not the most placid of relation
ships——' and what relationship with Sacha ever would

be? she wondered miserably '—but he loves her and he'll no doubt marry her.' She gave a weary shake of her head as Jill made to protest. 'I'm not quoting the gossip columns . . . I'm quoting Sacha.'

Jill's face fell in horror, then she began struggling for words. 'But it doesn't make sense . . . leaving housekeeping money for you like that,' she flustered. 'I mean . . . it's so *domesticated*, for heaven's sake! And if he loves this ghastly Deborah so much, what's he been doing——?'

'Jill—please! This housekeeping money, as you call it . . . it's . . .' It was his final and most calculatingly cruel insult, she realised brokenly.

'I'm only going by his note,' protested Jill. 'I mean, what does he expect—that you'll hang around at his place waiting for him to come back . . . and possibly with this woman in tow?'

'Please, Jill, I . . . I can't think properly at the moment. I . . .' She broke off, the realisation that she would have to start thinking, and thinking hard and clearly, suddenly crashing into her consciousness. 'Jill, I've got to do something!' She leapt to her feet, distraught and agitated. 'I can't stay here—I can't possibly!'

'Cassie, calm down,' begged Jill, jumping from the desk and trying to place a comforting arm around her.

'You don't understand, Jill, I have to leave here . . . leave Carmichael's and leave Sacha's house . . . I can't possibly stay!'

Trying to mask her increasing concern, Jill urged her back on to the chair. 'Cassie, you can't possibly leave Carmichael's,' she pointed out gently. 'Your whole problem is money, and you'll never be able to match what you're earning here.'

'I know...but I can't stay,' whispered Cassandra brokenly. 'I'll just have to explain everything to the Maltons—the people whose house I was in...they were both close friends of my father's and I know I can stay there.'

'You'll stay at my place till we sort something out,' stated Jill firmly. 'It's small, but one of us can sleep on the sofa—— '

'No...I have to go round to the Maltons' anyway,' exclaimed Cassandra agitatedly, random irrelevancies chasing through her mind. 'They might have some post for me... I didn't get around to letting everyone know my new address.'

'All right, we'll go round there after work and then we'll go and get your things from Sacha's place. Cassie, you didn't want to tell these people the whole story before, and I really don't think you're up to telling them right now.' Jill knelt down beside Cassandra and took her hands in hers, squeezing them encouragingly. 'So you're staying at my place—no arguing. And tonight, if you're up to it, you'll ring your sister and tell her exactly how things stand. Cassie, half your trouble is that you've been too busy trying to protect too many people from the truth.'

'But not Sacha,' whispered Cassandra, her voice far away and her eyes lifeless in her tense face. 'It was myself I was protecting from the way Sacha would probably interpret the truth... If only he didn't have all that wealth... Charles has none, yet Helen still couldn't bring herself to tell him the truth...but I think I'd have been able to tell Sacha, if only he'd been poor like Charles.'

Trying desperately to mask her horror at what she regarded as dangerously disjointed rambling on Cassandra's part, Jill glanced quickly at her watch.

'Look, it's only twenty minutes to going-home time—how about if we just shut up shop now?' she suggested briskly. Her heart sank as Cassandra merely continued staring blankly into space. 'Right—we're going,' she announced decisively, and went to get their coats.

CHAPTER TEN

'CASSIE, if you don't keep trying you'll never catch Helen,' said Jill quietly, her heart going out to the slight figure sitting huddled in the large armchair opposite her.

'I did try,' sighed Cassandra, trying desperately to shake off the terrible lethargy possessing her and wondering if her mind would ever again be capable of sustaining a single coherent thought. 'She never seems to be in.'

'Twice in four days is hardly a record-breaking attempt,' chided Jill gently. 'Cassie, I know how you must be dreading it, but I'm sure you'll begin feeling the worst's behind you once you've got it over and done with.'

'That's what I keep telling myself... Just give me a few more minutes to finish psyching myself up, then I intend ringing her every hour on the hour until I get her.'

'I didn't mean to nag,' said Jill anxiously.

'You, nag?' asked Cassandra with a wan smile. 'Jill, you have the patience of a saint—I'm sure that had I been you I'd have washed my hands of myself days ago.'

'You're not by any chance referring to the clothes?' chuckled Jill, rolling her eyes.

'Not specifically,' murmured Cassandra, her eyes clouding. 'But you do understand about them...don't you?' she added diffidently. 'I mean, Sacha bought me far more clothes than could ever be put down just to smartening up my image as an employee.'

'Cassie, of course I understand that you'd feel obliged to leave them all behind,' soothed Jill. 'It's just that image *is* important—especially when you're out hunting for a job that carries the size of salary you've been getting at Carmichael's.'

Cassandra pulled a wry face. 'I suppose there's always the nightclub circuit ... Only joking,' she added, as Jill gave a groan of disbelief. 'I just wish I didn't know how right you are about image—it's absolutely imperative that I get something that pays well.'

'But once you've explained to Helen——'

'It won't alter the fact that I have to pay my share,' she cut in dejectedly. 'Otherwise Helen and I could end up old women before we're free!'

'Cassie, I understand, but you have to be realistic,' pleaded Jill.

'Talking of being realistic reminds me—if ever I do manage to get through to Helen, I'm paying for the call——'

'Cassandra!' groaned Jill. 'We've already been over all that! By the way, did you ever get round to reading that post you collected from the Maltons' the other night?'

'What a subtle change of topic,' teased Cassandra, reaching down for the handbag at her feet. 'Though it's a good job you mentioned it, I'd forgotten all about it.' She examined the three envelopes she took from her bag, pulling a small face as she did so. 'I've a nasty suspicion they're all from the same place—my bank.'

She opened one of the envelopes, frowning to see a cheque fall out. When she had read the accompanying letter, she leaned back wearily in the chair.

'Cassie?'

'I'm trying to decide whether to laugh or to cry,' she groaned in answer to Jill's look of alarm. 'They've bounced one of my cheques...the one I paid for Sacha's dry-cleaning with!'

'Why on earth were you paying for Sacha's dry-cleaning?' demanded Jill in bewilderment. 'But before you answer that—don't you think you should see if they've bounced any others?' she added anxiously, indicating the two unopened envelopes.

Cassandra checked. 'No—these are just moans about the unhealthy state of my account,' she reported with a sigh of relief.

She was halfway through explaining when she noticed the date the cheque had been refused, and it was then that things began falling into place in her mind. The morning Sacha had returned to work after being ill, he had been relaxed and friendly. It hadn't been until that evening that he had reverted to cold cynicism and then to haranguing her about her finances...later, and after he had had a chance to read what the postman had handed him on their way out of the house!

'Jill, I honestly thought he was just having a go at me in general,' she exclaimed. 'You know how it is once you start noticing something odd about someone—you notice every minute detail in connection with it. And he was bound to find it odd that I never had so much as the price of an evening newspaper on me... But I just hadn't dreamt there was something like this at the back of it.'

And who in his right mind would ever believe any intelligent woman would demean herself with the type of extra work she had taken on, merely in order to buy her sister a present? she demanded of herself accusingly.

'I'll make us a quick cup of tea,' said Jill, rising. 'Then we'll try getting through to your sister.'

Cassandra nodded, then leaned back and closed her eyes. There were so many things she should be thinking about right at this very moment—her imminent call to Helen, for one—yet her head was filled solely with images of Sacha: images so sharp she could almost feel his presence; almost smell the warm fresh scent of him in her nostrils and the madness-inducing touch of his skin against hers.

She hugged her arms protectively around herself, trying desperately to dispel those images, while a terrible desolation filled her with the knowledge that she would never be free of him.

'Here, drink this and stop fretting,' urged Jill, handing her a cup. 'It won't seem nearly as bad once you hear her voice—I'm sure she'll be in this time.'

Cassandra nodded, knowing Jill had misinterpreted her preoccupation, but guiltily grateful to leave it at that.

It wasn't until she had actually started dialling the number that the full implication of the blow she was about to deliver to her sister finally hit her. Poor Helen, she thought wretchedly, this was the last thing she needed!

It threw her completely when a man's voice answered the phone.

'Sorry—would you mind repeating the number?' she asked, though certain she had heard correctly.

'Is that you, Cassie?' asked that same soft American voice.

'Yes.'

'Cassie, it's Charles Maynard—remember me?'

'Yes . . . yes, of course I do. Charles, where's——?'

'Before you say anything,' he interrupted, his voice relaxed with laughter, 'you'd better hear our news first—we've been trying to track you down since yesterday. . .'

Jill remained seated, finishing off her tea. She had considered taking herself off to the kitchen while Cassandra spoke to her sister, but it was Cassandra's obviously vulnerable emotional state that had decided her against it. And now she watched with a mixture of anxiety and bemusement the rapid succession of differing expressions chasing across Cassandra's pale features.

Whoever it was on the other end of the line was doing a great deal of talking, she thought anxiously—Cassandra was saying barely a word.

'Charles...I...I can't find any words to tell you how happy I am for you both...and as for the other...' stammered Cassandra, the tears choking her words to a halt, bringing Jill leaping to her feet with the sudden terrible thought that something might have happened to Helen. 'Yes...I can't wait to speak to Helen.'

When she heard those words, Jill returned to her armchair with an audible sigh of relief.

Cassandra's words, even to her own ears, sounded disjointed and senseless. And when she finally replaced the receiver she stumbled back to her seat, her mind a daze of bewilderment and tears streaming down her cheeks.

'Jill, there's nothing to worry about, I promise you,' she choked, suddenly aware of how she must be appearing.

'You just get your breath back,' said Jill calmly, then went to the small drinks cabinet in the corner of the room and poured two brandies. 'Have a few sips of that,' she urged, handing one to Cassandra and then returning to her chair.

Cassandra took a gulp, wincing as the pungent warmth of the brandy caught the back of her throat.

'Jill, I honestly don't know where to begin,' she whispered dazedly. 'Perhaps if I explain about Charles and Helen first... My mind's simply not up to taking in the rest for the moment.'

She took a deep breath and then, with complete honesty, related everything concerning her father's uncompromising attitude to the few men with whom Helen had been involved. She told of Charles Maynard and of his return into Helen's life all these years later. And by the time she had got round to her distressing previous conversation with her sister, tears were already welling in Jill's eyes.

'But that was Charles you spoke to first, wasn't it?' choked Jill. 'So he obviously wasn't prepared to accept Helen's refusal to see him again.'

'Actually, she didn't see him for the next two days,' replied Cassandra. 'Because Charles was off doing a bit of detective work.'

'He found out about the money owed to the hospital?'

Cassandra nodded. 'It was only because he'd got it out of her that she loved him that he felt free to pry. And, of course, once he knew he went straight back to her and all hell was let loose. As Helen had always suspected he would, he insisted that by his going into a more lucrative branch of medicine he would be able to clear the debt.'

'The last thing Helen wanted!' groaned Jill.

Cassandra nodded. 'She would agree to marry him only on condition that he remained doing the work he loved. Charles gave in, but only after imposing a condition of his own—that we now split the debt three ways.'

'Oh, Cassie, that's wonderful!' exclaimed Jill. 'And not only for Helen and Charles—now you won't have nearly as much to contribute!'

'That's the part I'm still having difficulty taking in,' whispered Cassandra, her voice strained. 'I shan't have anything to contribute any more.'

'Cassie... I'm afraid you've lost me,' stammered Jill, flashing her an anxious look.

'Yesterday the hospital contacted Helen to tell her the debt had been paid off in full—and by that I mean we're also to be reimbursed every cent we've contributed so far.'

'But who paid it, for heaven's sake?' gasped Jill.

'A wealthy admirer of Dad's—that's all they'd tell Helen.'

'Heavens, no wonder you're having difficulty taking it in,' breathed Jill. 'It's like a fairy-tale!'

'Yes, it is,' murmured Cassandra. 'Especially since Charles and Helen are to be married on New Year's Day.'

'You will be going over for the wedding, won't you?' asked Jill quietly, detecting the empty bleakness of pain still lingering in Cassandra's eyes despite the animation now accentuating her gentle beauty.

Cassandra nodded. 'They're telexing my bank the refund and some extra to cover the fare and to tide me over until I've straightened out my finances here...but I'll pay them back, of course,' she added hastily, bringing a chuckle from Jill.

'I'm beginning to realise how well I've got to know you,' Jill said softly. 'You're very proud—almost touchy—when it comes to money...and Helen sounds just the same.'

'It's only because we haven't any,' sighed Cassandra.

'I'm sure that if Charles had had the money he'd have paid off your debt,' mused Jill. 'But I suppose your sister wouldn't have told him even if he'd been a Rockefeller.'

'No, she probably wouldn't have,' agreed Cassandra, eyeing her questioningly.

'I was just wondering how Sacha would have reacted...had he known,' said Jill quietly.

'Sacha has a conviction that all a woman wants from him is his money,' Cassandra stated tonelessly, adding hastily, 'Well, obviously not Deborah.' She ignored Jill's sceptical look. 'And besides, the reason Charles would have paid, had he had the means, is that he happens to love Helen.'

Wanting to kick herself for the look of brooding desolation her thoughtless words had brought to her friend's face, Jill quickly changed the subject.

'All this is bound to put a new light on your future plans. Have you thought what you'll do now?'

'It still hasn't really sunk in yet,' sighed Cassandra. 'But the fact remains that I still have to find myself a job, and somewhere to live right away. I'll only be going over to the States for a few days for the wedding, but I'd like to have a job lined up to come back to. I could perhaps get temporary work—in a shop, or somewhere—until Christmas.'

'I'm going to my parents in Devon over Christmas—you're very welcome to join us.'

'Jill, that's very sweet of you,' choked Cassandra, shaking her head and praying she wasn't about to make a fool of herself yet again. 'But——'

'You don't have to come to any decision right now,' chided Jill gently. 'And if you'd really rather be on your own, at least you'll have this place to yourself. It's pointless even considering finding somewhere else to stay—wait until you've sorted out a job.'

'Jill, I honestly don't know what I'd have done without a friend like you,' muttered Cassandra. 'And I also honestly never believed I could turn into one of those pathetic types who start blubbing every five minutes,' she added, scrubbing frustratedly at her glistening cheeks.

'Cassie, with what you've been through recently, I'd say there'd be grounds for concern if you didn't have the odd blub now and then,' Jill told her easily.

'But now that ghastly millstone of debt's no longer round my neck, you'd think I'd be...that...' She broke off, screwing her eyes tightly shut. 'Jill, do me a favour and pretend I'm not here for a couple of minutes, will you?' she begged.

'Oh, my poor Cassie,' whispered Jill sadly. 'You might have been freed from your debt, but only time will ever free you from Sacha.'

Cassandra nodded, while in her heart she knew there would never come a time when she would be free from him; perhaps all she could hope for was a day when her body would no longer burn with the craving it now constantly did for the sweet, wild loving of his.

'Cassie, I know he's the last person you want mentioned right now, but I have to know what you want me to say to him on Monday.'

Cassandra opened her eyes, her expression momentarily blank. 'You don't have to tell him anything, Jill,' she said quietly. 'I've already sent my letter of resignation, which he'll get on Monday...if he's back by then, that is.'

'Of course he'll be back!' exclaimed Jill. 'He's not the type to hare off and leave his business unattended for long!'

'Except that he'll have Deborah's wishes to consider from now on,' pointed out Cassandra, partially to test her own reaction to that stark piece of reality—and finding it every bit as unbearable as she had dreaded.

'Well, I'm prepared to bet he'll be back—he'll have had the best part of a week away,' insisted Jill. 'In any case, it wasn't your resignation I was thinking about. He's bound to want to know where you are, Cassie.'

'I doubt it,' retorted Cassandra. Her going would come as a blessing to him, she informed herself grimly, especially as she couldn't envisage Deborah not returning with him. 'But if he does...' She hesitated.

'Cassie, do you want him to know where you are, or not?'

Cassandra shook her head violently. 'But I can't expect you to lie for me, Jill,' she protested.

'Rest assured,' declared Jill grimly, 'that's one lie I'll tell without the slightest compunction!'

'According to Lisa, all hell broke loose the moment he read your letter,' announced Jill, letting herself into the flat only minutes after Cassandra had returned from an entire day spent registering at employment agencies. 'And it remained rampaging on the loose for the remainder of the time he was in the building,' she added, her eyes scrutinising Cassandra's wooden features.

'And I dare say that wasn't for very long,' muttered Cassandra, finishing off the tea she had been making. 'He'd have Deborah to rush home to.'

Jill removed her coat. 'Quite frankly, I wouldn't fancy being anyone he was rushing home to, the mood he was

in,' she sighed. 'Though mood's not the right word—
Cassie, he was in a complete state when he ordered me
into his office.'

Every nerve in Cassandra's body tensed. 'He knows
perfectly well you're capable of running the
Tower——'

'Cassie, don't let's kid ourselves. He knows as well as
we do that I'm capable of no such thing! I'd have no
idea how to handle all those academics without you to
guide me.'

'But you know I'll always give you whatever help you
need,' protested Cassandra, disturbed by something she
was unable to define in Jill.

'And anyway, that's not what he wanted to see me
about,' said Jill. 'Cassie, he was desperate to know where
you are—he's worried out of his mind!'

'Jill, you didn't——'

'No—I didn't,' sighed Jill, getting the milk from the
fridge.

'I knew I hadn't the right to ask you to lie for me,'
said Cassandra miserably.

'Cassie, I told you I'd do it without compunction,'
Jill pointed out. 'It's just...Cassie, I don't think I've
ever seen a man quite as desperate as Sacha was today.'

Cassandra poured the tea and handed her a cup, her
heart thudding painfully.

'Hasn't it occurred to you that Deborah has probably
decided to give him a taste of his own medicine by playing
hard to get?' she exploded in sudden bitterness. 'Jill, all
I ask is to be left alone to get on with my own life,' she
pleaded, the explosion subsiding in her as swiftly as it
had erupted.

'I know that,' replied Jill with a remorseful sigh. 'So
tell me, how did you get on today?'

*   *   *

As she had the previous night, Jill returned home close on Cassandra's heels.

'Sacha said to tell you he'd be at home tonight, should you decide to see sense,' she announced as Cassandra greeted her.

Cassandra hung up her coat in silence, playing for time to gather her scattered wits and racked by guilt that she had asked Jill to lie for her in the first place.

'No, Cassie, I didn't spill the beans, if that's what you're wondering,' said Jill gently. 'He gave me that message straight after he'd fired me.'

'He what?' shrieked Cassandra, flying into the living-room after Jill. 'Jill, this is ludicrous—he can't just fire you like that!'

'You try telling Sacha that,' suggested Jill, her expression oddly verging on amusement. 'Our new-found ally Lisa suspects that he went round and gave your friends the Maltons the third degree.'

'Oh, heavens, no!' groaned Cassandra.

'And I've a feeling she may be right . . . and that they no doubt described the person you were with the other night.'

'But how on earth can he fire you? This has absolutely nothing to do with your ability to do your job!' protested Cassandra, completely outraged. 'It's out-and-out victimisation!'

'Whatever it is—I've been sacked,' said Jill, grinning.

Cassandra looked at her untroubled face with complete bemusement. Then she gave a soft groan as the truth hit her: Jill was putting on this brave face solely for her benefit!

'We'll see about that,' she muttered grimly, marching to the hall and putting back on the raincoat she had just removed.

'Cassie, where are you going?' enquired Jill.

'Sacha had as little right to fire you as I had to drag you into all this,' Cassandra stated firmly. 'I'm going to get you your job back!'

Giving Jill no time to reply, she raced from the flat, and it was the burning rage of fury in her that shielded her from the harsh bite of the evening air as she made her journey.

He was an utterly unprincipled monster! she raged. All right, there was that one, infinitesimal thread of gentleness in him, but the rest was rotten through and through. Cold and manipulative, he hadn't even had the perspicacity to recognise the love she had handed him with such open and reckless indiscretion. And even now, when he was discarding her, he was prepared to do it on no other terms but his own. There was to be no slinking off for her to lick her wounds in private—oh, no, Sacha would insist that every 'I' be dotted and every 'T' crossed before he tidied her away, and God help anyone foolish enough to try getting in his way!

Fuelled by the abundance of such thoughts, the rage burned on in her, its fierce heat undiminished and still cloaking her in its impenetrable protection when she eventually rang the doorbell of the house she had once shared with the demon so engrossing her every thought.

'How dare you?' she demanded, her rage boiling over now that he was at last before her. 'You think you can use people and just toss them aside, and if they should have the temerity to refuse to jump to your every command they're tossed aside even more quickly!' Suddenly she found herself running out of steam—and with terrifying swiftness. 'You...you can't just fire Jill like——'

'Cassandra, shriek at me like a fishwife if that's what you want, but I'd rather you came inside and did it,' Sacha drawled disdainfully.

'If you're worried about what your neighbours think, you——' Her words were cut short in a startled yelp as he grabbed her by the arm and yanked her inside.

'I don't give a damn what my neighbours think, I just happen to find it uncomfortably cold with the door open... Now, what can I do for you?'

It was the friendly enveloping warmth of the house, that faint aroma of polished wood and those other indefinable yet familiarly welcoming smells, that continued the rapid erosion of the cloak of her protection. But it was the stifling intensity of the strength of the yearnings aroused in her at the sight of the man now gazing down at her from watchful, waiting eyes that stripped the last shreds of that protection from her.

'Why did you sack Jill?' she asked, her hoarse words barely audible as her treacherous heart deserted her in a riotous tumult of joy at his presence.

'Because it was the only ploy I could think of that would guarantee bringing you here,' he replied without any trace of guilt. 'Cassie, why don't you take off your coat and come into the living-room? We have to talk.'

She shook her head, the terrible realisation coming to her of exactly what her reckless dash round here had left her open to... Any moment Deborah would appear.

'No! I have to go! Sacha, I know I haven't the right to ask anything of you... but please... please don't fire Jill.'

'Jill stays fired until you and I have spoken—so it's up to you, Cassandra.'

'But why? What can we possibly have to talk about?' she blurted out as reason seemed to desert her. 'And what about Deborah?'

For an instant his entire body seemed to freeze, then he ran his fingers through his hair in a jerky, almost nervous movement.

'Cassandra, what the hell has Deborah got to do with anything?' he demanded, his head shaking as though in disbelief.

'Everything!' she flung wildly at him, past caring how much her desperate outbursts might reveal. 'She's the woman you love! The one you went all the way to America to—— Let go of me!' she protested frantically as he got her by the arms and frog-marched her into the sitting-room.

'Cassandra, calm down, will you?' he snapped, urging her down on to the sofa. 'I think it's about time we indulged in some of that plain speaking you claim to be so at ease with, yet run a mile from whenever it so suits you,' he informed her harshly, towering over her. 'So—we'll start with Deborah. What on earth gave you the idea I was in love with the woman?'

'You did! You *told* me you were!'

'I did?'

'You can mock all you like,' she declared wearily. 'But you also told me you'd probably marry her.'

'I told you no such thing,' he rasped impatiently. 'Your trouble is that you don't bother listening to what's being said to you!'

'I *did* listen, and I understood perfectly,' she retorted angrily, a completely sane part of her refusing to accept that this ridiculous conversation was taking place.

'Cassandra, what you heard was my quoting to you what the gossip columns were claiming . . . So you didn't listen, and you most certainly didn't understand.'

'Split hairs all you like,' she muttered stiffly. 'But you did go to America after her.'

He rammed his hands in his pockets and scowled down at her. 'Do you intend continuing with this fascinating script you're concocting, or am I to be allowed to disrupt it with a few facts?'

'Feel free to disrupt,' she retorted recklessly. 'It's what you're best at!'

'That's rich—coming from you!' he exploded furiously. 'Cassandra, you wished me luck on my trip . . . are you now telling me it was in finding Deborah?' The look on his face was one of complete outrage. And it was as though weak from that same outrage that he flung himself heavily down on the dainty carved coffee-table behind him. 'God almighty—I don't believe this!'

'Well, I did wish you luck,' she muttered, distracted by her conviction that the table was about to collapse beneath his weight.

'Why?'

'Why what?' she groaned. She was having enough problems with the confusion in her mind without his adding to them.

'Why did you wish me luck with Deborah?'

'Because . . .' She broke off, jumping agitatedly to her feet.

'Cassandra, for heaven's sake sit down,' he pleaded wearily, rising. 'And for God's sake take off that bloody coat!'

'Why?' she demanded angrily. 'So that you can lecture me on how ghastly what's under it looks?'

'No. So that I shan't have to stand guard over you to prevent you racing off—that's why!'

'I'm not racing off anywhere,' she muttered defeatedly, returning to the sofa and unbuttoning her coat. 'Not until I know Jill has her job back...and because I owe you an apology. I'm sorry for all the embarrassment it must have caused you when my cheque bounced. I wish you'd told——'

'Cassandra, you can bounce cheques from here to kingdom come—that's not the problem.'

'You may not think so, but I——'

'Cassandra, are those the only reasons you're staying, the bounced cheque and Jill's job?'

'I can't think of any other,' she replied stiffly.

'Perhaps I can give you a few,' he suggested, walking over to one of the armchairs and flinging himself down on it. 'Such as my reason for dashing off to the States as I did.'

'I'm all ears,' she retorted, her attempt at sarcasm failing miserably, as did her attempts at willing herself to hate him.

'So was your sister—and Charles Maynard...a man I have much in common with, it would seem.'

'You saw Charles and Helen?' she croaked, convinced her mind was seizing up on her. 'When?'

'On Sunday... Why hadn't you the sense to let them know where you were staying?'

'I...this has nothing to do with your going to the States,' she stalled, in an attempt to recover her wits.

'Hasn't it?' he rasped. 'You weren't prepared to tell me the truth, so what option had I but to go and find it out for myself?'

'You ... you actually went there ... just to dig up what dirt you could on me?' she whispered, her words filled with horror.

His face was mask-like as his eyes searched out hers. 'I had no idea what I was likely to find ... but it wasn't dirt I went looking for, I can assure you.'

'But that's what you found, isn't it, Sacha?' she asked wearily. 'That, as you'd once so rightly accused me of being, I was up to my eyeballs in debt. But did you find it *all* out?' she demanded, unable to stem the terrible tide of bitterness now flowing from her. 'That someone who happened to admire my father has now paid everything off?'

'Yes,' he growled, his eyes trained on his fingers drumming restlessly on the arm of his chair.

Stunned, but with her bitterness still unspent, she lashed out again. 'And what makes you think you could possibly have anything in common with Charles Maynard?'

'The fact that, like me, he was forced to find out for himself,' he snapped, jerking to his feet and striding over to her. 'And, like me, he would have gladly paid fifty times the debt had he had the means!' He reached out and grasped her, hauling her to her feet and into his arms. 'Can you believe me when I say that, Cassandra ... that I'd have gladly paid it all and much more?' he demanded, the last of his words barely coherent as his mouth closed hungrily over hers.

Her arms were around his neck, her hands and fingers searching and tracing in familiar places while her lips gave themselves without hesitation to his.

'Where were you all day?' he groaned. 'I rang Jill's number God knows how many times!'

'Sacha, please... Sacha, stop this, will you?' she cried, willing her uncooperative arms to free him. 'I can't think straight! You keep jumping from one thing to another before I can——'

'But you don't have to think, not here in my arms, do you, Cassie?' he pleaded huskily against her parted lips. 'Just tell me you don't love me... tell me!'

Even had she been a thousand miles from him, instead of in the intoxicating hold of his arms, and even had her mind not been reduced to the state of total confusion it now was, she could never have uttered the lie he demanded of her.

He drew back slightly from her, his eyes blazing down into hers. 'Tell me you don't love me,' he demanded yet again.

'Sacha...you're confusing me,' she protested weakly. 'Comparing yourself to Charles... saying you'd gladly have paid all that money... you couldn't have meant it!'

'All right, if that's what you want—I was joking,' he muttered impatiently. 'Now, let's go to bed.'

Humiliation imbuing her with a strength she would never otherwise have possessed, she tore herself from his arms.

'You're sick, and I hate you!' she hurled at him in outrage.

'Why, because I suggest we go to bed?' he retaliated savagely. 'Can't you understand that it's only when we're making love that I've ever felt sure of getting an honest response from you... and hell, even then, how could I be absolutely sure?'

'Because even then I might go and spoil it all by telling you how much I love you, is that it?' she shrieked at him. 'Well, let me spoil it without your having to go to the trouble of bedding me! I love you! I never wanted your rotten money—never! I just made the fatal mistake of loving you!'

'Cassie, don't,' he groaned, catching her to him. 'The problem between us had nothing to do with money—can't you understand that?' he whispered distractedly. 'You mean more than all the money in the world to me. I had to clear your debt because I love you, not from any ulterior motive!'

'I beg your pardon?' she croaked—her senses once more deserting her completely.

'Oh, hell!' he groaned savagely, burying his face against her. 'Why do you always make me say things I have no intention of saying?'

'Are you telling me you didn't mean it?' she protested weakly, the shaky stirrings of what might have been happiness whipped from her before she could even ascertain what they might have been.

'What's the use of lying?' he asked wearily. 'It's the lack of the truth that's always been the wedge between us... Yes, I paid the damned hospital, and I'd have——'

'I'm not interested in that,' she cut in, her words peculiarly strained. That fleeting feeling had returned, now positively recognisable as the onslaught of happiness; and suddenly neither the debt, nor who had paid it, nor anything else to do with it, mattered.

'Cassie, you've got to give me a chance,' he pleaded, his arms tightening fiercely. 'You've admitted you love me, for God's sake!'

'Yes, but I'd like to discuss something far more important than that wretched debt right now.'

'You would?' he croaked dazedly.

'Yes, I would,' she murmured, resolutely freeing herself from his suffocating hold.

'Cassie? What the hell are you doing?'

'I'm taking off my disgusting raincoat . . . so that I can put my arms round you properly.'

Though his astounded look told her he thought she was completely out of her mind, he welcomed her back into his arms with uninhibited enthusiasm.

'Your raincoat's beautiful,' he said diffidently, then immediately gave a groan of exasperated bewilderment. 'Look, would you mind doing all the talking from now on? I haven't the slightest idea what's going on . . . not that I'm lodging any complaints.'

'You did say that you love me . . . didn't you?' she demanded tremulously.

'Of course I damned well love you! No man in his right mind would carry on as I've been unless he was completely and irrevocably in love!' he exclaimed indignantly. 'Cassie—now what are you doing?'

'I think I'm having a mental breakdown!' she sobbed furiously. 'How can you just come out with . . . with something like that and not expect me to . . . to . . . ? Oh, heck, this is so humiliating!'

'Cassie, I'm sorry,' he whispered, drawing her down on to the sofa and cradling her to him. 'Do you really believe that, if it had just been a matter of telling you I loved you, I wouldn't have? Be honest—if I'd told you last week, what would you have done?' he asked, his fingers gently stroking away her tears.

'I'd have probably have run a mile, but only because——'

'Of that wretched secret you and your equally infuriating sister have been so determinedly keeping to yourselves,' he finished for her. 'Darling, I might have had no idea what it was, but I sure as hell knew it existed and that it was jeopardising our every chance of love. I tried everything I could to get it out of you...and in all the wrong ways.'

'There were times I was almost tempted to tell you,' she whispered. 'But with your attitude to women and money——'

'Cassie, when a man starts sounding as extreme as I must have to you, it's a sure bet he's putting up every defence he can against falling in love!' he exclaimed.

'But you meant what you said about your brother.'

'Yes...because I was afraid he was in danger of making the same mistake I almost did when I was a couple of years younger than he is now,' he sighed. 'But Max is a far more level-headed character than I ever was, and I simply had no right to judge him by my past mistakes.' He gave a groan of frustration. 'Past mistakes—who am I kidding? Cassie, no one could possibly have made a more appalling hash of being in love than I have with you!'

'But I loved you, despite it,' she whispered, love pounding through her with a breathtaking joy. 'You must always have known that.'

'Must I have?' he whispered, burying his face against hers. 'Cassie, one of the reasons I've always behaved so badly towards you is that I've never been completely sure of anything with you. How could you have taken off as you did?' he protested hoarsely. 'I rang and rang here from the States—I was going out of my mind when there was no reply! The only reason I tracked down your sister was to find out if she knew where you were.'

'Did you tell her it was you who had paid off the debt?'

'No, of course I didn't! All I wanted was to find out where you were. And I managed to make such a spectacle of myself that they were left in no doubts as to how much I love you. Cassie, why did you take off like that?'

'I thought you loved Deborah,' she whispered, burying her face against him.

He drew her firmly from him, a burning intensity in his eyes as he gazed down at her.

'Cassie, you're the only woman I've ever really loved,' he vowed ardently. 'Deborah's...hell, Deborah's just Deborah. I enjoyed her sense of humour until it backfired on me. I never had any feelings even approaching love for her.'

'How do you mean—backfired?' she demanded, lifting her face.

'She started talking about moving in with me...I didn't take her seriously, just as I didn't take seriously what I took to be her joking threat of a lawsuit until too late,' he muttered uncomfortably. 'I had no intention of having anything to do with her when she came back to London, even though she told me she was dropping the lawsuit. But she gave me a heart-wrenching story about her sister being desperately ill and how she needed a friend. I began to have my suspicions when the Press just happened to turn up in their droves on the couple of occasions we had a meal together...then I found out about her sister and sent her packing.'

'Wasn't her sister really ill?' asked Cassandra.

'Well, she was in hospital, as Deborah had claimed— but only to have cosmetic surgery,' he explained wryly. 'Then, as before, I've never really fathomed out what it was Deborah was actually up to,' he added with a puzzled sigh.

'You're not very good at telling when a woman's in love with you,' she chided softly.

'I very much doubt if Deborah's in love with anyone but herself,' he laughed. 'But as for you...I'd forgotten how love can befuddle the mind——'

'You've just told me I'm the only woman you've ever really loved!' she interrupted indignantly, happiness now a beautiful, lazy warmth within her.

'Yes...well, you see,' he hedged, grinning down at her, 'woman she wasn't—I was about twelve at the time, and I think she was ten,' he laughed, hugging her to him. 'And, what's more, she didn't respond to my proposal of marriage quite as I'd hoped.'

'How did she respond?' chuckled Cassandra, freeing herself to entwine her arms round his neck.

'She fell about the place laughing. So tell me, my sweet, beautiful Cassie...how are you about to respond?'

Her eyes locked in the silent questioning of his, she opened her mouth, but no sound came.

'At least you're not laughing,' he whispered huskily. 'But the question still remains—will you be my wife?'

'Sacha, I...do you really want to marry me?' she croaked, her mind floating off on a cloud and refusing her every effort to bring it back.

'No, I was addressing that bird on your shoulder,' he groaned impatiently. 'Cassie, of course I want to marry you, I want it more than I've ever wanted anything in my life before!'

'Oh, Sacha, of course I will, I——'

'How about on New Year's Day in Boston?'

'I...you...oh, Sacha, I love you so much!' she wailed, pressing her cheek to his and clinging tightly to him.

'Cassie, you're throttling me!' he gasped. 'And you haven't told me if New Year's Day is OK with you.'

'Of course it is!' she shrieked. 'Do you mean...with Helen and Charles?'

'Yes,' he whispered huskily. 'Your very canny sister did happen to mention a sixth sense telling her the Lestor girls could well end up having a double wedding if I played my cards right. Needless to say, with the state I was in at the time, I regarded her as being out of her mind; so we'd better ring Boston...but perhaps we ought to ring Jill first. Cassie, do you think a trip to our wedding would help make up for the terrible way I bullied that poor girl today?'

She drew back from him, love spilling over in her as she gazed into his eyes. 'I hope so, because you realise you fired one of your brightest employees today, when you fired her?'

'I did?' he teased, his lips nuzzling lazily against her cheek.

'Yes. Because she didn't seem in the least put out about losing her job—almost pleased, in fact.'

'Because she saw what you couldn't?' he chuckled. 'That I was a man out of my mind with love...and Mrs E's just as bright, because she got the same message, though you'd have to have witnessed it to believe the callousness with which that woman has treated me since you abandoned me. Perhaps we'd better ring her too— I hate being in her bad books.'

'Sacha, I still haven't even thanked you for paying off my father's debt!' she exclaimed in sudden horror.

'Well, don't—because I warn you, if you do I might just get nasty and decide to deduct it from your house-keeping,' he murmured, nibbling her ear.

'You told the hospital authorities you were an admirer of his...but I know you disapproved of his methods——'

'Cassie, no matter what I think, he was the father of the woman I love above all else,' he chided softly.

Caught between tears and laughter, she turned slightly. 'Sacha, I think you'd better pinch me,' she whispered tremulously against his lips. 'Because I don't believe it's possible for anyone to feel as happy as I do at this very moment.'

'Why—because you've just saved on your house-keeping, or because Mrs E's been treating me so heartlessly?' he teased.

'It's . . . it's just because,' she gasped distractedly as his hands began weaving their familiar magic.

'Cassie, I've already pinched myself and the feeling didn't disappear,' he murmured huskily, a trembling impatience now in his hands. 'And I really think we ought to get those phone calls made . . . so that I can then start proving to you that we'll be resorting to pinching ourselves like this on and off for the rest of our lives.'

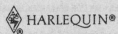

The most romantic day of the year is here! Escape into the exquisite world of love with MY VALENTINE 1993. What better way to celebrate Valentine's Day than with this very romantic, sensuous collection of four original short stories, written by some of Harlequin's most popular authors.

**ANNE STUART
JUDITH ARNOLD
ANNE McALLISTER
LINDA RANDALL WISDOM**

**THIS VALENTINE'S DAY, DISCOVER ROMANCE
WITH MY VALENTINE 1993**

Available in February wherever Harlequin Books are sold. VAL93

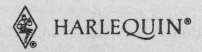

HARLEQUIN®

THE TAGGARTS OF TEXAS!

Harlequin's Ruth Jean Dale brings you
THE TAGGARTS OF TEXAS!

Those Taggart men—strong, sexy and hard to resist...

You've met Jesse James Taggart in FIREWORKS!
Harlequin Romance #3205 (July 1992)

And Trey Smith—he's THE RED-BLOODED YANKEE!
Harlequin Temptation #413 (October 1992)

Now meet Daniel Boone Taggart in SHOWDOWN!
Harlequin Romance #3242 (January 1993)

And finally the Taggarts who started it all—in LEGEND!
Harlequin Historical #168 (April 1993)

Read all the Taggart romances!
Meet all the Taggart men!

Available wherever Harlequin Books are sold.

HARLEQUIN ✦ PRESENTS®

A Year
DOWN UNDER

In February, we will take you to Sydney, Australia, with
NO GENTLE SEDUCTION by Helen Bianchin,
Harlequin Presents #1527.

Lexi Harrison and Georg Nicolaos move in the right
circles. Lexi's a model and Georg is a wealthy Sydney
businessman. Life seems perfect . . . so why have they
agreed to a *pretend* engagement?

Share the adventure—and the romance—
of A Year Down Under!

Available this month in
A YEAR DOWN UNDER

HEART OF THE OUTBACK
by Emma Darcy
Harlequin Presents #1519
Wherever Harlequin books are sold.   YDU-J